### "Take a deep breath," he instructed. "It'll help."

She did as he told her, which was when Ethan realized that his supporting arm was way too close to her chest. As she inhaled, her breasts rose, making contact with his forearm.

All sorts of responses went ricocheting through Ethan.

"Am I getting to you, Detective O'Brien?"

"Lady, we're way past 'getting' and hip-deep into 'got,' as in you 'got to me.'"

Sensing she was about to fall, Ethan tightened his hold around her waist, dragging her closer against him.

For one second, their faces were less than a measurable inch away from one another.

Giving in to the moment, Kansas kissed him.

Ethan let himself enjoy what was happening. The kiss packed a wallop that left him breathless, shaken and wa
Definitely more.

**\*\***

AUTHOR'S **200**th BOOK

Dear Reader,

So here we are with another Cavanaugh story. By all rights, this is also the last one. And if you believe that, you don't know me. I have a great deal of trouble letting go, except for a truly awful experience. In essence, I am an emotional pack rat.

Case in point: when I was a teenager in New York City, every year we had a real Christmas tree. I would plead for our tree to stay well into January and once, actually into February (Valentine bush, anyone?). As with everything else, it had been a source of joy once and I didn't want to let it go. So how could I possibly say goodbye to a family I have come to love?

Sidebar: this is my two hundredth book with Silhouette and the mother company, Harlequin Books. Not bad for a person who thought she had only one, possibly two books in her when she started out. I have loved every nail-biting minute and hope to write another two hundred!

As ever, thank you for reading my books, and from the bottom of my heart I wish you someone to love who loves you back.

Marie Ferrarella

AUTHOR'S 200th BOOK

# MARIE FERRARELLA

*Cavanaugh Reunion*

# ROMANTIC

*SUSPENSE*

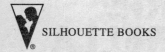

SILHOUETTE BOOKS

Recycling programs
for this product may
not exist in your area.

ISBN-13: 978-0-373-27693-6

CAVANAUGH REUNION

Copyright © 2010 by Marie Rydzynski-Ferrarella

All rights reserved. Except for use in any review, the reproduction
or utilization of this work in whole or in part in any form by any
electronic, mechanical or other means, now known or hereafter
invented, including xerography, photocopying and recording, or in
any information storage or retrieval system, is forbidden without
the written permission of the editorial office, Silhouette Books,
233 Broadway, New York, NY 10279 U.S.A.

This is a work of fiction. Names, characters, places and incidents are
either the product of the author's imagination or are used fictitiously, and
any resemblance to actual persons, living or dead, business establishments,
events or locales is entirely coincidental.

This edition published by arrangement with Harlequin Books S.A.

For questions and comments about the quality of this book
please contact us at Customer_eCare@Harlequin.ca.

® and TM are trademarks of Harlequin Books S.A., used under license.
Trademarks indicated with ® are registered in the United States Patent
and Trademark Office, the Canadian Trade Marks Office and in other
countries.

Visit Silhouette Books at www.eHarlequin.com

**Printed in U.S.A.**

**Books by Marie Ferrarella**

---

## MARIE FERRARELLA

This *USA TODAY* bestselling and RITA® Award-winning author has written two hundred books for Silhouette and Harlequin Books, some under the name of Marie Nicole. Her romances are beloved by fans worldwide. Visit her Web site at www.marieferrarella.com.

To
the wonderful Silhouette/Harlequin family,
and especially Patience Smith,
who more than lives up to her name.
I thank you all for making my dreams come true.
Also, to Pat Teal,
who started it all by asking,
"Would you like to write a romance?"
Thank God I said, "Yes."
And last, but by no means least,
to you, beloved readers,
thank you!
I wouldn't be here without
you.

# Chapter 1

He smelled it before he saw it.

His mind elsewhere, Detective Ethan O'Brien's attention was immediately captured by the distinct, soul-disturbing smell that swept in, riding the evening breeze. Without warning, it maliciously announced that someone's dreams were being dashed even as they were being burnt to cinders.

Or, at the very least, they were damaged enough to generate a feeling of overwhelming sorrow and hopelessness.

Summers in California meant fires, they always had. Natives and transplants would joke that fires, earthquakes and mudslides were the dues they paid for having the best, most temperate overall weather in the country. But they only joked when nothing was burning, shaking or sliding away. Because during these catastrophic events, life proved to be all too tenuous, and there was no time for humor, only action. Humor was a salve at best, before and after the fact. Action was a way to hopefully curtail the amount of damage, if at all humanly possible.

But it wasn't summer. It was spring, and ordinarily, devastating fires should have still been many headlines away from becoming a very real threat.

Except that they were a real threat.

There were fires blazing all over the southern section of Aurora. Not the spontaneous fires that arose from spurts of bone-melting heat, or because a capricious wind had seized a not-quite-dead ember and turned it into something lethal by carrying it off and depositing it into the brush. These fires, ten so far and counting in the last two months, were man-made, the work of some bedeviled soul for reasons that Ethan had yet to understand.

But he swore to himself that he would.

He'd been assigned to his very first task force by Brian Cavanaugh, the Aurora Police Department's chief of detectives, and, as he'd come to learn in the last nine months, also his paternal uncle.

Knowledge of the latter tie had jolted him, Kyle and Greer the way nothing ever had before. He could state that for a fact, seeing as how, since they were triplets, there were times when he could swear that they functioned as one, single-minded unit.

The three of them received the news at the same time. It had come from their mother in the form of a deathbed confession so that she could meet her maker with a clear conscience. She'd died within hours of telling them, having absolutely no idea what kind of turmoil her revelation had caused for him and his siblings.

Initially, finding out that he, Kyle and Greer were actually part of the sprawling Cavanaugh family had shaken the very foundations of their world. But in the end, once they'd gotten used to it and accepted the truth, the information had proven not to be life-shattering after all.

He had to admit, at least for him, that it was nice to be part of something larger than a breadbox. Back when his mother's death was still imminent, he'd anticipated life being pared down to it being just the three of them once she was gone. Three united against the world, so to speak.

Instead, the three of them were suddenly part of a network, part of something that at times seemed even greater than the sum of its parts.

Just like that, they were Cavanaughs.

There were some on the police force who were quick to cry "Nepotism!" when he, Kyle and Greer advanced, rising above the legions of patrol officers to become detectives in the department. But as he was quick to point out when confronted, it was merit that brought them to where they were, not favoritism.

Merit riding on the shoulders of abilities and quick thinking.

Like now.

On his way home after an extraordinarily long day that had wound up slipping its way into the even longer evening, Ethan had rolled his windows down in an attempt to just clear his head.

Instead, it had done just the opposite.

It felt as if smoke were leeching its way into his lungs and body through every available pore. The starless sky had rendered the black smoke all but invisible until he was practically on top of it.

But nothing could cover up the acrid smell.

In the time that it took for the presence of smoke from the fire to register, Ethan was able to make out where the telltale smell was emanating from. The building to his right on the next block was on fire. Big-time.

Ethan brought his lovingly restored 1964 Thunderbird sports car to a stop, parking it a block away so he didn't block whatever fire trucks were coming in. And truth be told, it was also to safeguard against anything happening to it. After his siblings, he loved the car, which he'd secretly named Annette, the most.

"I'll be right back, Annette," he promised the vehicle as he shut down the engine and leaped out. Despite the urgency of the situation, Ethan made sure that he locked the car before leaving it.

Where was everyone?

There were no fire trucks, not even a department car. People from the neighborhood were gathering around, drawn by the drama, but there was no indication of any firefighters on the scene.

But there was screaming. The sound of women and children screaming.

And then he saw why.

The building that was on fire was a shelter, specifically a shelter for battered women and their children.

Protocol, since there was no sign of a responding firehouse, would have him calling 911 before he did anything else. But protocol didn't have a child's screams ringing in its ears, and calling in the fire would be stealing precious seconds away from finding that child, seconds that could very well amount to the difference between life and death.

Out of the corner of his eye, Ethan saw several people gathering closer, tightening the perimeter of the so-called spectacle.

Voyeurs.

Disasters attracted audiences. This one time he used that to his advantage. Or rather the shelter's advantage.

"Call 911," he yelled to the man closest to him. "Tell them that the Katella Street Shelter's on fire." He had to shout the end of his sentence, as he was already running toward the building.

Turning his head to see if the man had complied, Ethan saw that he was just staring openmouthed at the building. Disgusted, Ethan reached into his pocket and pulled out his cell phone.

The fire couldn't be called an inferno yet, but he knew how little it took to achieve the transformation. It could literally happen in a heartbeat.

Raising the windbreaker he was wearing up over his head as a meager protective barrier against the flames, Ethan ran into the building even as he pressed 911.

The next moment, he stumbled backward, losing his footing as someone came charging out of the building. Springing up to his feet, Ethan saw that he'd just been knocked down by a woman. A small one at that. The blonde was holding an infant tucked against her chest with one arm while she held a toddler on her hip on the other side. A third child, just slightly older than the toddler, was desperately trying to keep up with her gait. He was holding tightly on to the bottom of her shirt and screaming in fear.

Trying to catch his breath, Ethan was torn between asking the woman if she was all right and his initial intent of making sure that everyone was out of the building.

The once run-down building was spewing smoke and women in almost equal proportions. In the background, Ethan heard the sound of approaching sirens. It was too soon for a response to the call he'd made. It was obvious to him that someone else must have already called this fire in. There were two firehouses in Aurora, one to take care of the fires in the southern portion, the other to handle the ones in the northern section. Even given the close proximity of the southern-section fire station, the trucks had to have already been on their way when he'd first spotted the fire.

The woman who had all but run over him now passed him going in the opposite direction. To his amazement, she seemed to be running back into the burning building.

Was she crazy?

He lost no time heading her off. "Hey, wait, what about your kids?" he called out. She didn't turn around to acknowledge that she'd heard him. Ethan sped up and got in front of her, blocking her path. "Have you got another one in there?" Ethan grabbed the woman's arm, pulling her away from the entrance as two more women, propping each other up, emerged. "Stay with your children," he ordered. "I'll find your other kid," he promised. "Just tell me where."

"I don't know where," she snapped as she pulled her arm free.

The next moment, holding her arm up against her nose and mouth in a futile attempt to keep at least some of the smoke at bay, the woman darted around him and ran back into the burning building.

Ethan bit off a curse. He had a choice of either remaining outside and letting the approaching fire-fighters go in after her or doing it himself. Seeing as how they had yet to pull up in front of the building, by the time they could get into the building, it might be too late. His conscience dictated his course for him. He had no choice but to run after her.

Ethan fully intended to drag the woman out once he caught up to her. If she was trying to find another one of her children, he had the sinking feeling that it was too late. In his opinion, no one could survive this, and she had three children huddled together on the sidewalk to think about.

Mentally cursing the fate that had him embroiled in all this, Ethan ran in. He made his way through the jaws of the fire, its flames flaring like sharp yellow teeth threatening to take a chunk out of his flesh. Miraculously, Ethan saw the woman just up ahead of him.

"Hey!" he shouted angrily. "Stop!"

But the woman kept moving. Ethan could see her frantically looking around. He could also see what she couldn't, that a beam just above her head was about to give way. Dashing over, his lungs beginning to feel as if they were bursting, Ethan pulled the woman back just as the beam came crashing down. It missed hitting her by a matter of inches.

Still she resisted, trying to pull free of his grasp again. "There might be more," she shouted above the fire's loud moan. She turned away but got nowhere. Frustrated fury was in her reddened eyes as she demanded, "Hey! Hey, what are you doing?"

"Saving your kids' mother," Ethan snapped back. He threw the obstinate woman over his shoulder, appropriately enough emulating fireman style.

She was saying something, no doubt protesting or cursing him, but he couldn't hear her voice above the sounds of the fire. As far as he was concerned, it was better that way.

His eyes burned and his lungs felt as if they were coming apart. The way out of the building felt as if it were twice as far as the way in had been.

Finally making it across the threshold, he stumbled out, passing several firefighters as they raced into the building.

One of the firefighters stopped long enough to address him and point out the paramedic truck that was just pulling up.

"You can get medical attention for her over there," were the words that the man tossed in his direction as he hurried off.

"Let go of me!" the woman yelled angrily. When he didn't respond fast enough, she began to pound on his back with her fists.

For a woman supposedly almost overcome with smoke, Ethan thought, she packed quite a wallop. He was having trouble hanging on to her. When he finally set her down near the ambulance, Ethan instinctively stepped back to avoid contact with her swinging fists.

She all but fell over from the momentum of the last missed swing. Her eyes blazed as she demanded, "What the hell do you think you were doing?"

He hadn't expected a profusion of gratitude, but neither had he expected a display of anger. "Off the top of my head, I'd have to say saving your life."

"Saving my life?" she echoed incredulously, staring at him as if he'd just declared that he thought she were a zebra.

"You're welcome," Ethan fired back. He gestured toward the curb where two of the three children were sitting. The third was in another woman's arms. The woman was crying. "Now go see to your kids."

She stared at him as if he'd lost his mind. What the hell was he babbling about? "What kids?" she cried, her temper flaring.

"Your kids." Annoyed when she continued staring at him, Ethan pointed to the three children she'd had hanging off her as if she were some mother possum. "Those."

She glanced in the direction he was pointing. "You think—" Stunned and fighting off a cough that threatened to completely overwhelm her, Kansas Beckett found that she just couldn't finish her thought for a moment. "Those aren't my kids," she finally managed to tell him.

"They're not?" They'd certainly seemed as if they were hers when she'd ushered them out. He looked back at the children. They were crying again, this time clinging to a woman who was equally as teary. "Whose are they?"

Kansas shrugged. "I don't know. Hers, I imagine." She nodded toward the woman holding the baby and gathering the other two to her as best she could. "I was just driving by when I smelled the smoke and heard the screams." Why was she even bothering to explain her actions to this take-charge Neanderthal? "I called it in and then tried to do what I could."

Kansas felt gritty and dirty, not to mention that she was probably going to have to throw out what had been, until tonight, her favorite suit because she sincerely doubted that even the world's best dry cleaner could get the smell of smoke out of it.

Ethan gaped at what amounted to a little bit of a woman. "You just ran in."

She looked at him as if she didn't understand what his problem was. "Yeah."

Didn't this woman have a working brain? "What are you, crazy?" he demanded.

"No, are you?" Kansas shot back in the same tone. She gestured toward the building that was now a hive of activity with firemen fighting to gain the upper hand over the blazing enemy. "From the looks of it, you did the same thing."

Was she trying to put them on the same footing? He was a trained professional and she was a woman with streaks of soot across her face and clothes. Albeit a beautiful woman, but beauty in this case had nothing to do with what mattered.

"It's different," he retorted.

Kansas fisted her hands on her hips, going toe-to-

toe with her so-called rescuer. She absolutely hated chauvinists, and this man was shaping up to be a card-carrying member of the club.

"Why?" she wanted to know. "Were you planning on using a secret weapon to put the fire out? Maybe huff and puff until you blew it all out? Or did you have something else in mind?" she asked, her eyes dipping down so that they took in the lower half of his frame. Her meaning was clear.

He didn't have time for this, Ethan thought in exasperation. He didn't have time to argue with a bull-headed woman who was obviously braver than she was smart. His guess was that she probably had a firefighter in the family. Maybe her father or a brother she was attempting to emulate for some unknown reason.

Ethan frowned. Why was it always the pretty ones who were insane? he wondered. Maybe it was just nature's way of leveling the playing field.

In any case, he needed to start asking questions, to start interviewing the survivors to find out if they'd seen or heard anything suspicious just before the fire broke out.

And he needed, he thought, to have the rest of his team out here. While his captain applauded initiative, he frowned on lone-ranger behavior.

Moving away from the woman who was giving him the evil eye, Ethan reached into his pocket to take out his cell phone—only to find that his pocket was empty.

"Damn," he muttered under his breath.

He remembered shoving the phone into his pocket and feeling it against his thigh as he started to run into the burning shelter. He slanted a look back at the woman.

He must have dropped it when she knocked him down at the building's entrance.

Kansas frowned. "What?"

Ethan saw that she'd bitten off the word as if it had been yanked out of her throat against her will. For a second, he thought about just ignoring her, but he needed to get his team out here, which meant that he needed a cell phone.

"I lost my cell phone," he told her, then added, "I think I must have lost it when you ran into me and knocked me down."

Ethan looked over in the general direction of the entrance, but the area was now covered with firefighters running hoses, weaving in and out of the building, conferring with other firemen. Two were trying to get the swelling crowd to stay behind the designated lines that had been put up to control the area. If his phone had been lost there, it was most likely long gone, another casualty of the flames.

"You ran into me," she corrected him tersely.

Was it his imagination, or was the woman looking at him suspiciously?

"Why do you want your cell phone?" Kansas asked him. "Do you want to take pictures of the fire?"

He stared at her. Why the hell would he want to do that? The woman really was a nut job. "What would anyone want their phone for?" he responded in annoyance. "I want to make a call."

Her frown deepened. She made a small, disparaging noise, then began to dig through her pockets. Finding her own phone, she grudgingly held it out to him.

"Here, you can borrow mine," she offered. "Just don't forget to give it back."

"Oh damn, there go my plans for selling it on eBay," he retorted. "Thanks," he said as he took the cell phone from her.

Ethan started to press a single key, then stopped himself. He was operating on automatic pilot and had just gone for the key that would have immediately hooked him up to the precinct. He vaguely wondered what pressing the number three on the woman's phone would connect him to. Probably her anger-management coach, he thought darkly. Too bad the classes weren't taking.

It took Ethan a few seconds to remember the number to his department. It had been at least six months since he'd had to dial the number directly.

He let it ring four times, then, when it was about to go to voice mail, he terminated the call and tried another number. All the while he was aware that this woman—with soot streaked across her face like war paint—was standing only a few feet away, watching him intently.

Why wasn't she getting herself checked out? he wondered. And why was she scrutinizing him so closely? Did she expect him to do something strange? Or was she afraid he was going to make off with her phone?

No one was picking up. Sighing, he ended the second call. Punching in yet another number, he began to mentally count off the number of rings.

The woman moved a little closer to him. "Nobody home?" she asked.

"Doesn't look that way."

But just as he said it, Ethan heard the phone on the other end being picked up. He held his hand up because she'd begun to say something. He hoped she'd pick up on his silent way of telling her to keep quiet while he was trying to hear.

"Cavanaugh," a deep voice on the other end of the line announced.

Great, like that was supposed to narrow things down. There were currently seventeen Cavanaughs on the police force—if he, Greer and Kyle were included in the count.

He thought for a moment, trying to remember the first name of the Cavanaugh who had been appointed head of this task force. Dax, that was it. Dax.

Ethan launched into the crux of his message. "Dax, this is Ethan O'Brien. I'm calling because there's just been another fire."

The terse statement immediately got the attention of the man he was calling—as well as the interest of the woman whose phone he was using.

# *Chapter 2*

"Give me your location," Dax Cavanaugh instructed. Then, before Ethan had a chance to give him the street coordinates, he offered, "I'll round up the rest of the team. You just do what you have to do until we get there."

The chief had appointed Dax to head up the team. Calling them was an assignment he could have easily passed on if he'd been filled with his own importance. But Ethan had come to learn that none of the Cavanaughs ever pulled rank, even when they could.

Ethan paused for a moment as he tried to recall the name of the intersection. When he did, he recited the street names, acutely aware that the woman to his right was staring at him as if she were expecting to witness some kind of a rare magic trick. Either that or she was afraid that he was going to run off with her cell phone.

"You want to call the chief, or should I?" Dax was asking, giving him the option.

Ethan thought it just a wee bit strange that Dax was referring to his own father by his official title, but he supposed that just verified the stories that the Cavanaughs went out of their way not to seem as if they were showing any favoritism toward one of their own.

"You can do it," Ethan told him. "The chief's most likely home by now, and you have his private number."

Ethan shifted to get out of the way. The area was getting more and more crowded with survivors from the shelter and the firemen were still fighting the good fight, trying to contain the blaze and save at least part of the building.

"And you don't?" Dax asked in surprise.

Out of the corner of his eye, Ethan saw the woman moving in closer to him. Apparently, she had no space issues. "No, why should I?"

"Because you're family," Dax said, as if Ethan should have known that. "My father lets everyone in the family have his home number." To back up his claim, Dax asked, "Do you want it?"

Dax began to rattle off the numbers, but Ethan stopped him before he was even halfway through. "That's okay, I'm going to have my hands full here until the rest of the team comes. You can do the honors and call him."

The truth of it was, Ethan didn't want to presume, no matter what Dax said to the contrary, that he was part of the Cavanaugh inner circle. Granted, he had Cavanaugh blood running through his veins, but the way he came to have it could easily be seen as a source of embarrassment, even in this day and age. Until he felt completely comfortable about it, he didn't want to assume too much. Right now, he was still feeling his way around this whole new scenario he found himself in and wanted to make sure he didn't antagonize either Andrew or Brian Cavanaugh.

Not that he would mind becoming a real part of the family. He wasn't like Kyle, who initially had viewed every interaction with their newfound family with suspicion, anticipating hostile rejection around every corner. He and his sister, Greer, secretly welcomed being part of a large, respected family after all the years they'd spent on the other side of the spectrum, poor and isolated—and usually two steps in front of the bill collector.

But he wanted to force nothing, take nothing for granted. If Brian Cavanaugh wanted him to have his private number, then it was going to have to come from Brian Cavanaugh, not his son.

"Will do," Dax was saying, and then he broke the connection.

The moment Ethan ended the call and handed the phone back to her, the blonde was openly studying him. "You a reporter?" she asked.

Damn, she was nosey. Just what was it that she was angling for? "No."

The quick, terse answer didn't seem to satisfy her curiosity. She came in from another angle. "Why all this interest in the fires?"

He answered her question with a question of his own. "Why the interest in my interest in the fires?" he countered.

Kansas lifted her chin. She was not about to allow herself to get sidetracked. "I asked first."

Instead of answering, Ethan reached out toward her hair. Annoyed, she began to jerk her head back, but he stopped her with, "You've got black flakes in your hair. I was just going to remove them. Unless you want them there," he speculated, raising a quizzical eyebrow and waiting for a response.

Something had just happened. Something completely uncalled-for. She'd felt a very definite wave of heat as his fingers made contact with her hair and scalp. Her imagination?

Kansas took a step back and did the honors herself, carelessly brushing her fingers through her long blond hair to get rid of any kind of soot or burnt debris she might have picked up while she was hustling the children out of the building. She supposed she should count herself lucky that it hadn't caught fire while she was getting the children out.

"There," she declared, her throat feeling tight for reasons that were completely beyond her. She tossed her head as a final sign of defiance. And then her eyes narrowed as she looked at him. "Now, why are you so interested in the fires, and who did you just call?"

She was no longer being just nosey, he thought. There was something else at work here. But what? Maybe she was a reporter and that was why she seemed to resent his being one, as per her last guess.

If that was what she was, then she was out of luck. Nothing he disliked more than reporters. "Lady, just because I borrowed your phone doesn't entitle you to my life story."

She squared her shoulders as if she were about to go into battle. He braced himself. "I don't want your life story. I just want an answer to my question, and it's Kansas, not 'lady.'"

Ethan's eyebrows lifted in confusion. What the hell was she talking about? "What's Kansas?"

Was she dealing with a village idiot, or was he just slow? "My name," she emphasized.

Ethan cocked his head, trying to absorb this meandering conversation. "Your last name's Kansas?"

She sighed. She was fairly certain he was doing this on purpose just to annoy her. "No, my *first* name is Kansas, and no matter how long you attempt to engage in this verbal shell game of yours, I'm not going to get sidetracked. Now, who did you call, and why are you so taken with this fire?" Before he could say anything, she asked him another question. "And what did you mean by 'there's been another one'?"

"The phrase 'another one' means that there's been more than one." He was deliberately goading her now. And enjoying it.

She said something under her breath that he couldn't quite make out, but he gathered it wasn't very favorable toward him.

"I know what the phrase means," she retorted through gritted teeth. "I'll ask you one more time—why are you so interested in the fires?"

"What happens after one more time?" Ethan wanted to know, amused by the woman despite himself. Irritating women usually annoyed the hell out of him—but there was something different about this one.

She drew herself up to her full height. "After one more time, I have you arrested."

*That* surprised him. "You're a cop?" He thought he knew most of the people on the force, by sight if not by name. He'd never seen her before.

"No. I'm a fire investigator," she informed him archly. "But I can still have you arrested. Clapped in irons would be my choice," Kansas added, savoring the image.

"Kinky," he commented. Damn, they were making fire investigators a hell of a lot prettier these days. *If* she was telling the truth. "Mind if I ask to see some identification?"

"And just so I know, who's asking?" she pressed, still trying to get a handle on his part in all this.

It was a known fact that pyromaniacs liked to stick around and watch their handiwork until the object of their interest burnt down to the ground and there was nothing left to watch. Since she'd begun her investigations and discovered that the fires had been set, Kansas had entertained several theories as to who or what was behind all these infernos. She was still sorting through them, looking for something that would rule out the others.

"Ethan O'Brien," he told her. She was still looking at him skeptically. He inclined his head. "I guess since you showed me yours, I'll show you mine." He took out his ID and his badge. "Detective Ethan O'Brien," he elaborated.

Like his siblings, he was still debating whether he was going to change his last name the way Brian and his brother Andrew, the former chief of police and reigning family patriarch, had told them they were welcome to do.

He knew that Greer was leaning toward it, as were Brian's four stepchildren who'd become part of the family when he married his widowed former partner. Kyle was the last holdout if he, Ethan, decided to go with the others. But he, Greer and Kyle had agreed that it would be an all-or-nothing decision for the three of them.

As for himself, he was giving the matter careful consideration.

"*You're* a cop," she concluded, quickly scanning the ID he held up.

"That I am," Ethan confirmed, slipping his wallet back into his pocket. "I'm on the task force investigating the recent crop of fires that have broken out in Aurora."

"They didn't just 'break out,'" she corrected him. "Those fires were all orchestrated, all set ahead of time."

"Yes, I know," Ethan allowed. He regarded her for a moment, wondering how much she might have by way of information. "How long have you been investigating this?"

There was only one way to answer that. "Longer than you," she promised.

She seemed awfully cocky. He found himself itching to take her down a peg. Take her down a peg and at the same time clean the soot off her bottom lip with his own.

*Careful, O'Brien,* he warned himself. *If anything, this is a professional relationship. Don't get personally involved, not even for a minute.*

"And you would know this how?" he challenged her. How would she know what was going on in his squad room?

"Simple. The fire department investigates every fire to make sure that it wasn't deliberately set," she answered him without missing a beat. "That would be something you should know heading into *your* investigation."

He'd never been one of those guys who felt superior to the softer of the species simply because he was a man. In his opinion, especially after growing up with Greer, women were every bit as capable and intelligent as men. More so sometimes. But he'd never had any use for people—male or female—who felt themselves to be above the law. Especially when they came across as haughty.

"Tell me," he said, lowering his voice as if he were about to share a secret thought. "How do you manage to stand up with that huge chip on your shoulder?"

Her eyes hardened, but to his surprise, no choice names were attached to his personage. Instead, using the same tone as he just had, she informed him, "I manage just fine, thanks."

"Kansas!" The fire chief, at least a decade older than his men and the young woman he called out to, hurried over to join them. Concern was etched into his features. "Are you all right?"

She flashed the older man a wide smile. "I'm fine, Chief," she assured him.

The expression on the older man's face said that he wasn't all that sure. "Someone said you ran into the burning building." He gestured toward the blazing building even as he leaned over to get a closer look at her face. "They weren't kidding, were they?"

She shrugged, not wanting to call any more undue attention to herself or her actions. "I heard kids screaming—"

Chief John Lawrence cut her off as he shook his head more in concern than disapproval. "You're not a firefighter anymore, Kansas," he pointed out. "And you should know better than to run into a burning building with no protective gear on."

She smiled and Ethan noted that it transformed her, softening her features and in general lighting up the immediate area around her. She was one of those people, he realized, who could light up a room with her smile. And frost it over with her frown.

It was never a good idea to argue with the fire chief. "Yes, I do, and I promise to do better next time," she told him, raising her hand as if she were taking an oath. "Hopefully, there won't be a next time."

"Amen to that," the chief agreed wholeheartedly. He had to get back to his men. The fire wasn't fully contained yet. "You stay put here until things are cool enough for you to conduct your initial investigation," he instructed.

The smile had turned into a grin and she rendered a mock salute in response to the man's attempt at admonishing her. "Yes, sir."

"Father?" Ethan asked the moment the chief had returned to his truck and his men.

Kansas turned toward him. He'd clearly lost her. "What?"

"Is the chief your father?" The older man certainly acted as if she were his daughter, Ethan thought.

Kansas laughed as she shook her head. "Don't let his wife hear you say that. No, Captain Lawrence is just a very good friend," she answered. "He helped train me, and when I wanted to get into investigative work, he backed me all the way. He's not my dad, but I wouldn't have minded it if he were."

At least, Kansas thought, that way she would have known who her father was.

His curiosity aroused, Ethan tried to read between the lines. Was there more to this "friend" thing than met the eye? Lawrence was certainly old enough to be her father, but that didn't stop some men. Or some women, especially if they wanted to get ahead.

"Friend," Ethan echoed. "As in boyfriend?" He raised an eyebrow, waiting to see how she'd react.

She lifted her chin. "Unless you're writing my biography, you don't have the right to ask that kind of question," she snapped.

Ethan's smile never wavered. He had a hunch that this woman's biography did *not* make for boring reading. "I'm not writing your biography," he clarified. "But there are some things I need to know—just for the record."

She bet he could talk the skin off a snake. "All right. For the 'record' I was the first one on the scene when the shelter began to burn—"

He'd already figured that part out. "Which is why I want to question you—at length," he added before she could brush the request aside. "I need to know if you saw anyone or anything that might have aroused your suspicions."

"Yes," she deadpanned, "I saw the flames—and I instantly knew it was a fire."

He had nothing against an occasional joke, but he resented like hell having his chain yanked. "Hey, 'Kansas,' in case it's escaped you, we're both on the same team. It seems to me that means we should be sharing information."

She was sure that he was more than eager for her to "share" and doubted very much that it would be a two-way street as far as he was concerned. Until he brought something to the table other than words, she was not about to share anything with him.

"Sorry." With that, she pushed past him.

"I bet the box that said 'works and plays well with others' always had 'needs improvement' checked on it," he said, raising his voice as she walked away.

She looked at him over her shoulder. "But the box labeled 'pummels annoying cop senseless' was also checked every time."

Ethan shook his head. Working together was just going to have to wait a couple of days. He had a definite hunch that she'd be coming around by then.

"Your loss," he called after her and turned just as he saw Dax Cavanaugh coming toward him.

Right behind him were Richard Ortiz and Alan Youngman, two other veteran detectives on the force who now found themselves part of the arson task force. Remarkably, none of the men seemed to resent his presence despite the fact that they were all veterans with several years to their credit, while this was his very first assignment as a detective.

There were times he could have sworn that his shield was still warm in his wallet.

"What have you got?" Ortiz asked him, looking more than a little disgruntled. "And it better be worth it because I was just about to get lucky with this hot little number."

"He doesn't want to hear about your rubber doll collection," Youngman deadpanned to his partner.

Ortiz looked insulted. "Hey, just because you're in a rut doesn't mean that I am," the younger man protested.

"Guys," Dax admonished in a low voice. "Playtime is over."

Youngman frowned as he shook his head. "You're no fun since they put you in charge."

"We'll have fun after we catch this arsonist and confiscate his matches," Dax replied.

Overhearing, Kansas couldn't help crossing back to the men and correcting this new detective. "He's not an arsonist."

Dax turned to her. His eyes, Ethan noticed, swept over the woman as if he were taking inventory. What was conspicuously missing was any indication of attraction. Brenda must be one hell of a woman, Ethan couldn't help thinking about the man's wife.

"And you would know this how?" Dax asked the self-proclaimed fire investigator.

"An angel whispered in her ear," Ethan quipped. "Dax, this is Kansas Beckett. She says she's the fire department's investigator. Kansas, this is Dax Cavanaugh, Alan Youngman and Richard Ortiz." Three heads bobbed in order of the introductions.

It was more information than she wanted, but she nodded at each man, then looked at the man conducting the introductions. "I didn't *say* I was the fire investigator. I *am* the fire investigator. And how did you know my last name?" she wanted to know. "I didn't give it to you."

"But remarkably, I can read," Ethan answered with an enigmatic smile. "And it was in on the ID you showed me"

"How do you know it's not an arsonist?" Dax persisted, more emphatically this time.

She patiently recited the standard differentiation. "Arsonists do it for profit," she told him, moving out of the way of several firefighters as they raced by, heading straight for the building's perimeter. "Their own or someone else's. The buildings that were torched, as far as we can ascertain, have no common thread drawing them together. For instance, there's no one who stands to profit from getting rid of a battered-women's shelter."

Ethan turned the thought over in his head. "Maybe there's a developer in the wings, looking to buy up land cheap in order to build a residential community or a king-sized mall or some vast hotel, something along those lines."

But she shook her head. "Too spread apart, too far-fetched," she pointed out. "It would have to be the biggest such undertaking in the country," she emphasized. "And I don't really think that's what's going on here."

Dax was open to any kind of a guess at this point. "So who or what do you think is behind these fires?" he asked her.

She was silent for a moment. Almost against her will, she glanced in Ethan's direction before answering. "My guess is that it's either a pyromaniac who's doing it for the sheer thrill of it, or we're up against someone with a vendetta who's trying to hide his crime in plain sight with a lot of camouflage activity."

"In which case, we have to find which is the intentional fire and which were set for show," Ethan theorized.

Kansas looked at him. "I'm impressed. Chalk one up for the pretty boy."

He couldn't tell if she was being sarcastic or actually giving him his due. With Kansas, he had a hunch that it was a little bit of both.

## Chapter 3

In all, twelve children and nineteen adults were saved. Because the firefighters had responded so quickly to Kansas's call—and despite the fact that several women and children wound up being taken to the hospital for treatment—not a single life was lost.

Tired, seriously bordering on being punchy, Ethan nonetheless remained at the scene with the other detectives, interviewing anyone who'd been in the building just before the fire broke out. It was a long shot, but he kept hoping that someone might have witnessed even the slightest thing that seemed out of the ordinary at the time.

Because she wanted to spare the victims any more unnecessary trauma, and since the nature of the questions that the police were asking were along the lines of what she wanted to ask, Kansas decided it was best to temporarily join forces with the Neanderthal who had slung her over his shoulder.

The women and children who'd been in the fire had her complete sympathy. She knew the horror they'd gone through. Knew, firsthand, how vulnerable and helpless they'd all felt. And how they'd all thought, at one point or another, that they were going to die.

Because she'd been trapped in just such a fire herself once.

When she was twelve years old, she'd been caught in a burning building. It occurred in the group home where she'd always managed to return. She came to regard it as a holding zone, a place to stay in between being placed in various foster homes. But in that case, there'd been no mystery as to how the fire had gotten started. Eric Johnson had disobeyed the woman who was in charge and not only played with matches but deliberately had set the draperies in the common room on fire.

Seeing what he'd done, Kansas had run toward the draperies and tried to put the fire out using a blanket that someone had left behind. All that had done was spread the flames. Eric had been sent to juvenile hall right after that.

Kansas couldn't help wondering what had happened to Eric after all these years. Was he out there somewhere, perpetuating his love affair with fire?

She made a mental note to see if she could find out where he was these days.

Kansas glanced at O'Brien. He looked tired, she noted, but he continued pushing on. For the most part, he was asking all the right questions. And for a good-looking man, he seemed to display a vein of sensitivity, as well. In her experience, most good-looking men didn't. They were usually one-dimensional and shallow, too enamored with the image in their mirror to even think about anyone else.

More than an hour of questioning yielded the consensus that the fire had "just come out nowhere." Most of the women questioned seemed to think it had started in the recreation room, although no one had actually seen it being started or even knew *how* it had started. When questioned further, they all more or less said the same thing. That they were just suddenly *aware* of the fire being there.

Panic had ensued as mothers frantically began searching for their children. The ones who hadn't been separated from their children to begin with herded them out into the moonless night amid screaming and accelerated pandemonium.

The chaos slowly abated as mother after mother was reunited with her children. But there was still one woman left searching. Looking bedraggled and utterly shell-shocked, the woman went from one person to another, asking if anyone had seen her daughter. No one had.

Unable to stand it any longer, Kansas caught O'Brien by the arm and pulled him around. She pointed to the hysterical woman. "She shouldn't have to look for her daughter on her own."

Busy comparing his findings with Dax and all but running on empty, Ethan nodded. "Fine, why don't you go help her." More than any of them, this impetuous, pushy woman seemed to have a relationship with the women at the shelter. At the very least, she seemed to be able to relate to them. Maybe she could pick up on something that he and the others on the task force couldn't—and more important, she could bring to the table what he felt was a woman's natural tendency to empathize. That would probably go a long way in giving the other woman some measure of comfort until they were able to hopefully locate her missing daughter.

Kansas pressed her lips together, biting back a stinging retort. She couldn't help thinking she'd just been brushed off.

*Not damn likely, Detective.*

Detective Ethan O'Brien, she silently promised herself, was about to discover that she didn't brush aside easily.

The moment she approached the distraught woman, the latter grabbed her by the arm. "Have you seen her? Can you help me find my Jennifer?"

"We're going to do everything we can to find her," Kansas told the woman as she gently escorted her over to one of the firemen. "Conway, I need your help."

"Anytime, Kansas. I'm all yours," the blond-haired fireman told her as he flashed a quick, toothy grin.

"This woman can't find her daughter. She might have been one of the kids taken to the hospital. See what you can do to reunite them," Kansas requested.

The fireman looked disappointed for a moment, then with a resigned shrug did as he was asked and took charge of the woman. "Don't worry, we'll find her," he said in a soothing, baritone voice.

Kansas flashed a smile at Conway before returning to O'Brien to listen in on his latest interview.

"Buck passing?" Ethan asked when she made her way

back to his circle. Curious to see what she did with the woman, he'd been watching her out of the corner of his eye.

"No," she answered tersely. "Choosing the most efficient path to get things done. Conway was part of the first team that made it inside. If there was anyone left to save, he would have found them." She crossed her arms. "He's also got a photographic memory and was there, helping to put the injured kids into the ambulances. If anyone can help find this woman's daughter, he can."

Ethan nodded, taking the information in. "You seem to know a lot about this Conway guy. You worked with him before?"

"For five years."

He was tempted to ask if she'd done more than just work with the man. The fact that the question even occurred to him caught him off guard. The woman was a barracuda. A gorgeous barracuda, but still a barracuda, and he knew better than to swim in the water near one. So it shouldn't matter whether their relationship went any deeper than just work.

But it did.

"How does someone get into that line of work?" he wanted to know.

He was prejudiced. It figured… "You mean how does a woman get into that line of work?"

Ethan knew what the sexy force of nature was doing, and he refused to get embroiled in a discussion that revolved around stereotypes. He had a more basic question than that. "How do you make yourself rush into burning buildings when everyone else is running in the opposite direction?"

It was something she'd never thought twice about. She'd just done it. It was the right thing to do. "Because you want to help, to save people. You did the very same thing," she pointed out, "and no one's even paying you to do it. It's not your job." She looked back toward Conway and the woman she'd entrusted to him. He was on the phone, most likely calling the hospital to find out if her daughter was there. Mentally, Kansas crossed her fingers for the woman.

"It's all part of 'protect and serve,'" she heard O'Brien telling her.

Kansas turned her attention back to the irritating detective with the sexy mouth. "If you understand that, then you have your answer."

Greer blustered through life, but Ethan's mother had been meek. He'd always thought that more women were like his mother than his sister. "Aren't you afraid of getting hurt? Of getting permanently scarred?"

Those thoughts had crossed her mind, but only fleetingly. She shook her head. "I'm more afraid of spending night after night with a nagging conscience that won't let me forget that I *didn't* do all I could to save someone. That because I hesitated or wasn't there to save them, someone died. There are enough things to feel guilty about in this world without adding to the sum total."

She didn't want to continue focusing on herself or her reaction to things. There was a more important topic to pursue. "So, did you find out anything useful?" she pressed.

What did she think she missed? "You were only gone a few minutes," he reminded her. The rest of the time, she'd been with him every step of the way—not that he really minded it. Even with soot on her face, the woman was extremely easy on the eyes.

"Crucial things can be said in less than a minute," she observed. Was he deliberately being evasive? *Had* he learned something?

"Sorry to disappoint you," Ethan said. "But nothing noteworthy was ascertained." He looked back at the building. The firemen had contained the blaze and only a section of the building had been destroyed. But it was still going to have to be evacuated for a good chunk of time while reconstruction was undertaken. "We'll know more when the ashes cool off and we can conduct a thorough search."

"That's my department," Kansas reminded him, taking pleasure in the fact that—as a fire investigator— her work took priority over his.

"Not tonight." He saw her eyes narrow, like someone getting ready for a fight. "Look, I don't want to have to go over your head," he warned her. He and the task force had dibs and that was that.

"And I don't want to have to take yours off," she fired back with feeling. "So back off. This is *my* investigation, O'Brien. Someone is burning down buildings in Aurora."

"And running the risk of killing people while he's doing it," Ethan concluded. "Dead people fall under my jurisdiction." And that, he felt, terminated the argument.

"And investigating man-made fires comes under mine," she insisted.

She didn't give an inch. Why didn't that surprise him?

"So you work together."

They turned in unison to see who had made the simple declaration. It had come from Brian Cavanaugh, the chief of police. When Dax had called him, Brian had lost no time getting to the site of the latest unexplained fire.

Brian looked from his new nephew to the woman Ethan was having a difference of opinion with. He saw not just a clash of temperaments as they fought over jurisdiction, but something more.

Something that, of late, he'd found himself privy to more than a few times. There had to be something in the air lately.

These two mixed like oil and water, he thought. And they'd be together for quite a while, he was willing to bet a month's salary on it.

His intense blue eyes, eyes that were identical in hue to those of the young man his late brother had sired, swept over Ethan and the investigator whose name he'd been told was Kansas. He perceived resistance to his instruction in both of them.

"Have I made myself clear?" Brian asked evenly.

"Perfectly," Ethan responded, coming to attention and standing soldier-straight.

Rather than mumble an agreement the way he'd expected her to, the young woman looked at him skeptically. "Did you clear this with the chief and my captain?"

"It was cleared the minute I suggested it," Brian said with no conceit attached to his words. "The bottom line is that we all want to find whoever's responsible for all this."

The expression was kind, the tone firm. This was a man, she sensed, people didn't argue with. And neither would she.

Unless it was for a good cause.

Kansas stayed long after the police task force had recorded and photographed their data, folded their tents and disappeared into what was left of the night. She liked conducting her investigation without having to trip over people, well intentioned or not. Gregarious and outgoing, Kansas still felt there was a time for silence and she processed things much better when there as a minimum of noise to distract her.

She'd found that obnoxious Detective O'Brien and his annoying smile most distracting of all.

Contrary to the fledgling opinion that had been formed—most likely to soothe the nerves of the shelter's residents—the fire hadn't been an accident. It had been started intentionally. She'd discovered an incendiary device hidden right off the kitchen, set for a time when the area was presumably empty. So whoever had done this hadn't wanted to isolate anyone or cut them off from making an escape. A fire in the kitchen when there was no one in the kitchen meant that the goal was destruction of property, not lives.

Too bad things didn't always go according to plan, she silently mourned. One of the shelter volunteers had gotten cut off from the others and hadn't made it out of the building. She'd been found on the floor, unconscious. The paramedics worked over the young woman for close to half an hour before she finally came around. She was one of the lucky.

Frowning, Kansas rocked back on her heels and shook her head.

This psychopath needed to be found and brought to justice quickly, before he did any more damage.

And she needed to get some sleep before she fell on her face.

She wondered where the displaced residents of the shelter would be sleeping tonight. She took comfort in the knowledge that they'd be returning in a few weeks even if the construction wasn't yet completed.

With a weary sigh, Kansas stood up and headed for the front entrance.

Just before she crossed the charred threshold, she kicked something. Curious, thinking it might just possibly have something to do with the identity of whoever started the fire, she stooped down to pick it up.

It turned out to be a cell phone—in pretty awful condition, from what she could tell. Flipping it open, she found that the battery was still active. She could just barely make out the wallpaper. It was a picture of three people. Squinting, she realized that the obnoxious detective who thought she needed to be carried out of the building fireman-style was in the photo.

There were two more people with him, both of whom looked identical to him. Now there was a curse, she mused, closing the phone again. Three Detective O'Briens. Kansas shivered at the thought.

"Tough night, huh?" the captain said, coming up to her. It wasn't really a question.

"That it was. On the heels of a tough day," she added. She hated not being able to come up with an answer, to have unsolved cases pile up on top of one another like some kind of uneven pyramid.

Captain John Lawrence looked at her with compassion. "Why don't you go home, Kansas?"

"I'm almost done," she told him.

His eyes swept over her and he shook his head. "Looks to me like you're almost done *in*." Lawrence nodded toward the building they'd just walked out of. "This'll all still be here tomorrow morning, Kansas. And you'll be a lot fresher. Maybe it'll make more sense to you then."

Kansas paused to look back at the building and sighed. "Burning buildings will never make any sense to me," she contradicted. "But maybe you're right about needing to look at this with fresh eyes."

"I'm always right," Lawrence told her with a chuckle. "That's why they made me the captain."

Kansas grinned. "That, and don't forget your overwhelming modesty."

"You've been paying attention." His eyes crinkled, all but disappearing when he smiled.

"Right from the beginning, Captain Lawrence," she assured him.

Captain Lawrence had been more than fair to her, and she appreciated that. She'd heard horror stories about other houses and how life became so intolerable that female firefighters wound up quitting. Not that she ever would. It wasn't in her nature to quit. But she appreciated not having to make that choice.

Looking down, she realized that she was even more covered with dust and soot than before. She attempted to dust herself off, but it seemed like an almost impossible task.

"I'll have a preliminary report on your desk in the morning," she promised.

Lawrence tapped her on the shoulder, and when she looked at him quizzically, he pointed up toward the sky. "It already is morning."

"Then I'd better go home and start typing," she quipped.

"Type later," Lawrence ordered. "Sleep now."

"Anyone ever tell you that you're a nag, Captain Lawrence?"

"My wife," he answered without skipping a beat. "But then, what does she know? Besides, compared to Martha, I'm a novice. You ever want to hear a pro, just stop by the house. I'll drop some socks on the floor and have her go at it for you." He looked at her. "I don't want to see you until at least midday."

"'O, Captain! my Captain!'" Throwing her wrist against her forehead in a melodramatic fashion, Kansas quoted a line out of a classic poem by Walt Whitman that seemed to fit here. "You've hurt my feelings."

He gave her a knowing look. "Can't hurt what you don't have."

"Right," she murmured.

She'd deliberately gone out of her way to come across like a militant fire investigator, more macho than the men she worked with. There was a reason for that. She didn't want to allow *anything* to tap into her feelings. By her reckoning, there had to be an entire reservoir of tears and emotions she had never allowed herself to access because she was sincerely afraid that if she ever did, she wouldn't be able to shut off the valve. It was far better never to access it in the first place.

Heading to her car, she put her hand into her pocket for the key…and touched the cell phone she'd discovered instead. She took it out and glanced down at it. She supposed that she could just drop it off at O'Brien's precinct. But he *had* looked concerned about losing the phone, and if she hadn't plowed into him like that, he wouldn't have lost the device.

Kansas frowned. She supposed she owed O'Brien for that.

She looked around and saw that there was still one person with the police department on the premises. Not pausing to debate the wisdom of her actions, she hurried over to the man. She was fairly certain that the chief of detectives would know where she could find the incorrigible Detective O'Brien.

"I could drop it off for you," Brian Cavanaugh volunteered after the pretty fire investigator had approached him to say that she'd found Ethan's cell phone.

She looked down at the smoke-streaked device and gave the chief's suggestion some thought. She *was* bone-tired, and she knew that the chief would get the phone to O'Brien.

Still, she had to admit that personally handing the cell phone to O'Brien would bring about some small sense of closure for her. And closure was a very rare thing in her life.

"No, that's all right. I'll do it," she told him. "If you could just tell me where to find him, I'd appreciate it."

"Of course, no problem. I have the address right here," he told her.

Brian suppressed a smile as he reached into his inside pocket for a pen and a piece of paper. Finding both, he took them out and began writing the address in large, block letters.

Not for a second had he doubted that that was going to be her answer.

"Here you go," he said, handing her the paper.

This, he thought, was going to be the start of something lasting.

## Chapter 4

Ethan wasn't a morning person, not by any stretch of the imagination. He never had been. Not even under the best of circumstances, coming off an actual full night's sleep, something that eluded him these days. Having less than four hours in which to recharge had left him feeling surly, less than communicative and only half-human.

So when he heard the doorbell to his garden apartment ring, Ethan's first impulse was to just ignore it. No one he knew had said anything about coming by at a little after six that morning. and it was either someone trying to save his soul—a religious sect had been making the rounds lately, scattering pamphlets about a better life to come in their wake—or the neighbor in the apartment catty-corner to his who had been pestering him with everything from a clogged drain to a key stuck in the ignition of her car, all of which he finally realized were just flimsy pretexts to see him. The woman, a very chatty brunette who wore too much makeup and too little clothing, had invited him over more than a dozen times, and each time he'd politely but firmly turned her down. By the time the woman had turned up on his doorstep a fifth time, his inner radar had screamed, "Run!" Two invitations were hospitable. Five, a bit pushy. More than a dozen was downright creepy.

When he didn't answer the first two rings, whoever was on his doorstep started knocking.

Pounding was actually a more accurate description of what was happening on the other side of his door.

Okay, he thought, no more Mr. Nice Guy. Whoever was banging on his door was going to get more than just a piece of his mind. He wasn't in the mood for this.

Swinging the door open, Ethan snapped, "What the hell do you want?" before he saw that it wasn't someone looking to guide him to the Promised Land, nor was it the pushy neighbor who wouldn't take no for an answer. It was the woman he'd met at the fire. The one, he'd thought, whose parents had a warped sense of humor and named her after a state best known for a little girl who'd gone traveling with her house and a dog named Toto.

"To give you back your cell phone," Kansas snapped back in the same tone he'd just used. "Here." She thrust the near-fried object at him.

As he took it, Kansas turned on her heel and started to walk away. *March away* was actually more of an accurate description.

It took Ethan a second to come to. "Wait, I'm sorry," he called out, hurrying after her to stop her from leaving. "I'm not my best in the morning," he apologized.

Now there was a news flash. "No kidding," she quipped, whirling around to face him. "I've seen friendlier grizzlies terrorizing a campsite on the Discovery Channel."

With a sigh, he dragged his hand through his unruly hair. "I thought you were someone else."

She laughed shortly. "My condolences to 'someone else.'" Obviously, it was true: no good deed really did go unpunished, Kansas thought.

But as she started to leave again, her short mission of reuniting O'Brien with his missing cell phone completed, the detective moved swiftly to get in front of her.

"You want to come in?" he asked, gesturing toward his apartment behind him.

Kansas glanced at it, and then at him. She was bone-weary and in no mood for a verbal sparring match. "Not really. I just wanted to deliver that in person, since, according to you, I was the reason you lost it in the first place."

Ethan winced slightly. Looking down at the charred device, he asked, "Where did you find it?"

"It was lying on the floor just inside the building." Because he seemed to want specifics, she took a guess how it had gotten there. "Someone must have accidentally kicked it in." She looked down at the phone. It did look pretty damaged. "I don't think it can be saved, but maybe the information that's stored on it can be transferred to another phone or something." She punctuated her statement with a shrug.

She'd done all she could on her end. The rest was up to him. In any case, all she wanted to do was get home, not stand here talking to a man wearing pajama bottoms precariously perched on a set of pretty damn terrific-looking hips. Their initial encounter last night had given her no idea that he had abs that would make the average woman weak in the knees.

The average woman, but not her, of course. She wasn't that shallow. Just very, very observant.

With effort, she raised her eyes to his face.

Ethan frowned at the bit of charred phone in his hand. They had a tech at the precinct who was very close to a magician when it came to electronic devices. If anyone could extract something from his fried phone, it was Albert.

"That's very thoughtful of you," he told her.

"That's me, thoughtful," Kansas retorted. It was too early for him to process sarcasm, so he just let her response pass. "Well, I'll see you—"

Ethan suddenly came to life. Shifting again so that he was once more blocking her path, he asked, "Have you had breakfast yet?"

Kansas blinked. "Breakfast?" she echoed. "I haven't had *dinner* yet." She'd been at the site of the women's shelter fire this entire time. And then she replayed his question in her head—and looked at him, stunned. "Are you offering to cook for me, Detective O'Brien?"

"Me?" he asked incredulously. "Hell, no." Ethan shook his head with feeling. "That wouldn't exactly be paying you back for being nice enough to bring this over to me. No, I was just thinking of taking someone up on a standing invitation."

And just what did that have to do with her? Kansas wondered. The man really wasn't kidding about mornings not being his best time. His thought process seemed to be leapfrogging all over the place.

"Well, you go ahead and take somebody up on that standing invitation," she told him, patting his shoulder. "And I'll—"

He cut her off, realizing he hadn't been clear. "The invitation isn't just for me. It applies to anyone I want to bring with me."

She looked at him. Suspicion crept in and got a toehold. Ethan O'Brien was more than mildly good-looking. Tall, dark, with movie-star-chiseled features and electric-blue eyes, he was the type of man who made otherwise reasonable, intelligent women become monosyllabic, slack-jawed idiots when he entered a room. But she'd had her shots against those kinds of men. She'd been married to one and swiftly divorced from him, as well. The upshot of that experience was that she only made a mistake once, and then she learned enough not to repeat it.

Her eyes narrowed. "Excuse me?"

"It's easier to show you. Wait here," Ethan told her, backing into the apartment. "I've just got to get dressed and get my gun."

"Now there's a line that any woman would find irresistible," she murmured to herself, then raised her voice as she called after him, "If it's all the same to you, Detective—" not that she cared if it was or not "—I'll just be on my way."

Ethan turned from his doorway, still very much underdressed. It was getting harder and harder for her to focus only on his face. "The invitation's for breakfast at my uncle's house," he told her. "Dozens of chairs, no waiting." The quote belonged to Andrew.

She had to admit that O'Brien had made her mildly curious. "What's he run, a diner?"

He had a feeling Andrew would have gotten a kick out of the question. "Very nearly. I've only been a couple of times," he confessed. "But the man's legend doesn't do him justice."

"I'm sure," she murmured. Ethan had the distinct feeling he was being brushed off. Her next words confirmed it. "But all I want to do right now is crawl into bed. If it's all the same to you, I'll just take a rain check."

Where this tinge of disappointment had come from was a complete mystery to him. He was only trying to thank her for reuniting him with his phone, nothing more. Ethan chalked it up to having his morning shaken up. "If I tell him that, he'll hold you to it. He'll expect you to come for breakfast sometime soon," Ethan added when she made no comment.

Like she believed that.

Kansas knew she should just let the matter drop, but it annoyed her that this walking stud of a detective thought she was naive enough to believe him. She deliberately pointed out the obvious.

"Your uncle has no idea who I am." And it was mutual, since she had no idea who this "Uncle Andrew" and his so-called legend were.

"Uncle Andrew's the former chief of police," O'Brien informed her. "He makes a point of knowing who *everyone* is when it comes to the police and fire departments."

This was something she was going to look into, if for no other reason than to be prepared in case she ever bumped into Detective Stud again.

"I consider myself duly warned," she replied. "Now, unless you want me falling asleep on your doorstep, I'm going to have to go."

Maybe not the doorstep, Ethan thought, but he certainly wouldn't mind finding her—awake or asleep—in his bed. He had a hunch, though, that she wouldn't exactly appreciate him vocalizing that right now.

"Sure. I understand. Thanks again," he said, holding up the phone she'd brought to him.

Kansas merely nodded and then turned and walked quickly away before O'Brien found something else he wanted to talk about. She headed toward the vehicle she'd left in guest parking.

Closing his hand over the charred phone, Ethan watched the sway of the fire investigator's hips as she moved. It was only when he became aware of the door of the apartment cattycorner to his opening that he quickly beat a hasty retreat before his neighbor stepped out and tried to entice him with yet another invitation. Last time she'd come to the door wearing a see-through nightgown. The woman spelled trouble any way you looked at it.

Andrew smiled to himself when he looked up to the oven door and saw the reflection of the man entering his state-of-the-art kitchen through the back door.

"C'mon in, little brother." Andrew turned from the tray of French toast he'd just drizzled a layer of powdered sugar on. His smile widened. He knew better than anyone how hectic and busy the life of a chief could be. "It's been a long time since you dropped by for breakfast." Maybe he was taking something for granted he shouldn't. "You *are* dropping by for breakfast, aren't you?"

Brian moved his shoulders vaguely, trying to appear indifferent despite the fact that the aroma rising up from his brother's handiwork had already begun making him salivate—and food had never been all that important to him.

"I could eat," he answered.

"If breakfast isn't your primary motive, what brings you here?" Andrew asked, placing two thick pieces of toasted French bread—coated and baked with egg batter, a drop of rum and nutmeg—onto a plate on the counter and moving it until it was in front of his brother.

Brian took the knife and fork Andrew silently offered. "I wanted to see if you'd gotten over it."

Andrew slid onto the counter stool next to his younger brother. "'It'?" he repeated in confusion. "Someone say I was sick?"

"Not sick," Brian answered, trying not to sigh and sound like a man who'd died and gone to heaven. His wife, Lila, was a good cook, but not like this. "Just indifferent."

Rather than being clarified, the issue had just gotten more muddied. "What the hell are you talking about, Brian?"

Brian's answer came between mouthfuls of French toast. He knew it was impossible, but each bite seemed to be better than the last.

"About not answering when someone calls to you."

He paused to look at his older brother. The brother he'd idolized as a boy. "Now, my guess is that you're either going deaf, or something's wrong."

Andrew frowned slightly. None of this was making any sense to him. "My hearing's just as good as it ever was, and if there's something wrong, it's with this so-called story of yours."

Putting down his fork, Brian looked around to make sure that his sister-in-law wasn't anywhere within earshot. He got down to the real reason he'd come. Lowering his voice, he said, "I came here to tell you to get your act together before it's too late."

This was just getting more and more convoluted. "Explain this to me slowly," he instructed his brother. "From the top."

Brian sighed, pushing the empty plate away. "I saw you with that woman."

"Woman?" Andrew repeated, saying the word as if Brian had just accused him of being with a Martian. "What woman? Where?" Before Brian could elaborate, Andrew cut in, concerned. He knew how hard Brian worked. "Brian, maybe it's time to start considering early retirement. We both know that this job can eat you alive if you let it. You have a lot to live for. Lila, your kids, Lila's kids—"

This time Brian cut Andrew off. "This has nothing to do with the job, and I'm well aware of my blessings. I'm just concerned that maybe you're taking yours for granted." He hated being his brother's keeper. Andrew was always the moral standard for the rest of them. But after the other day, he knew he had to say something. "I know what I saw."

Andrew sighed. "And what is it that you *think* you saw?"

*He's actually going to make me say it,* Brian thought, upset about having been put in this position. "You, walking into the Crystal Penguin, with another woman."

"The Crystal Penguin?" Andrew repeated incredulously. The Crystal Penguin was an overpriced restaurant that didn't always deliver on its promises of exquisite dining experiences. "Why would I go to a restaurant? And if I did go to one, it certainly wouldn't be a restaurant that overcharges and undercooks."

That's what he would have thought if someone had come to him with this story. But he'd been a witness to this. "I saw you, Andrew."

Andrew didn't waste his breath protesting that it wasn't possible. "And just when did this 'sighting' occur?"

Brian had been sitting on this for several days now, and it was killing him. "Last Friday evening. At about seven-thirty."

"I see." His expression was unreadable. "Why didn't you come up and talk to me?"

He almost had, then decided to restrain himself. "Because you're my older brother and I didn't want to embarrass you."

And then Brian delivered what in his estimation was the knockout blow.

"Some of the others have mentioned seeing you around the city with this woman. I told them they were crazy, but then on Friday I saw you myself, and now I'm begging you," he entreated, putting his hand on

Andrew's arm, "break it off before Rose gets hurt. You spent all that time looking for Rose when everyone else, including me, thought she was dead. Don't throw all that away because of some middle-aged itch you want to scratch."

"You done?" Andrew wanted to know.

"Yes," Brian said quietly. "Just promise me you'll break if off with her."

"It would seem like the thing to do." To Brian's surprise, his brother got off the stool, walked to the doorway between the kitchen and the living room and called out, "Rose? Would you mind coming here?"

Brian hurried over to him. "What are you doing?" he whispered into Andrew's ear. He knew that for some, the need to confess was almost an overpowering reaction, but he would have never thought it of Andrew. This had all the makings of a disaster. "Don't dump this on Rose. Don't tell her you've been cheating on her just to clear your conscience."

"Good advice," Andrew quipped.

Before Brian could ask if he'd lost his mind, Rose walked in. "Hello, Brian. Nice to see you." She turned toward her husband. There was no missing the love in her eyes. "You wanted me, honey?"

"Only every minute of every day," Andrew said, a gentle smile curving the corners of his mouth. He slipped his arm around her waist. "Rose, could you tell Brian where we were last Friday?"

Rose sighed, shaking her head. "Don't see why you would even want to admit to it."

He laughed, giving her a quick hug. "Humor me, my love."

"Okay." Rose turned toward her brother-in-law. "We saw the most god-awful movie. *Heaven Around the Corner.* Quite honestly, I still can't figure out how the people behind that silly thing managed to get funding to produce it." Her eyes crinkled as she slanted a glance and a grin in her husband's direction. "Even Andrew could have written a better story."

"Thank you, dear," Andrew deadpanned. "I can always count on you to extol my many talents."

She laughed. Standing on her toes, she brushed a kiss against his cheek. "Don't worry, dear. No one can touch your cooking."

Still holding his wife to him, Andrew turned his attention back to his younger brother and Brian's allegations. "Satisfied?"

Rose looked from one man to the other, a curious expression filling her eyes. "Satisfied about what? What's this all about, Andrew? Brian?" She waited for one of them to enlighten her.

"Brian thought he saw me clear across town last Friday. At the Crystal Penguin. With another woman. I don't know which is more absurd, the restaurant part or the other woman part." He caught the look on Rose's face. "The other woman part. Definitely the other woman part," he assured her.

Amused, Rose laughed. "Not unless Andrew's suddenly gotten superpowers and found a way to be in two places at the same time."

Brian sighed with relief. "You don't know how glad it makes me to hear that." But then he frowned slightly. There was still a mystery to be unraveled. "But whoever I saw looked just like you, Andrew."

"Maybe it was one of the boys," Andrew suggested.

But Brian shook his head. He'd already thought of that. "Too old."

Andrew gave him a quick jab in the arm. "Thanks a lot."

He hadn't meant it as an insult. "You know what I mean. Around our age, not younger."

"Someone else out there with those handsome features?" Rose teased, brushing her hand across her husband's cheek.

"I know. Lucky dog," Andrew deadpanned. He grew a little more serious as he asked Brian, "And you're saying this isn't the first time this doppelgänger's been spotted?"

Brian nodded. "Jared's mentioned seeing 'you,'" he told Andrew, referring to one of his sons. "Said you ignored him when he called out to you. And Zack said he thought he saw you walking into the Federal Building about a month ago. Same scenario. He called out and was ignored."

Listening to this, Rose glanced at her husband. He'd become quietly thoughtful. "I know that look," she said. "You're working something out in your head."

"What's on your mind?" Brian probed.

Andrew raised his eyes to look at Brian. "That maybe Mom wasn't imagining things all those years ago."

## Chapter 5

Still completely in the dark, Brian and Rose exchanged quizzical glances.

Brian was the first to speak. "Mom wasn't wrong about what?"

Andrew looked up as if he'd suddenly become aware that he wasn't alone and talking to himself. "That the hospital had given her the wrong baby." He doled out the words slowly, thoughtfully, as he continued sorting things out in his mind.

"The wrong baby?" Brian echoed, staring at Andrew as if his brother had just sprouted another head. This was making less sense now, not more. "Which one of us is supposed to have been this 'wrong baby'? Mike or me?"

Andrew took a deep breath before answering. It had been a very long time since the name he was about to say had been uttered. An entire lifetime had gone by. It had become a family secret, known to only his late parents and him. Maybe it was time to air out the closet.

"Sean."

"Sean?" Brian repeated, more mystified than ever. "Andrew, maybe you've been standing in the kitchen too long and the heat's gotten to you. I know that there are a lot of Cavanaughs to be tallied these days, but there is no Sean in our family."

"I know." Andrew's eyes met Brian's. "That's because he died."

Brian shook his head as if to clear it. It didn't help. "Andrew, what are you *talking* about?"

*In for a penny, in for a pound.* He needed to get this whole thing out. It was long overdue.

"Something Mother and Dad never wanted to talk about." He looked from his brother to his wife. "Sit down, Brian. You, too, Rose."

Rose dropped onto the counter stool beside her husband. "I think I'd better. Is this where you tell me I'm married to someone who's descended from the Romanovs?" she asked, clearly trying very hard to lighten the somber mood that was encompassing them.

Maybe he should have done this years ago, after their parents were both gone. But he'd always felt it wasn't his secret to share. And he'd been so young when it was all going down. There were times he had almost talked himself into believing it had all been just a dream.

"No, love." He felt her slip her fingers through his, as if silently offering him her support, no matter what was ahead. God, he loved this woman. "This is where I tell Brian that there were actually four Cavanaugh boys, not three."

None of this was making any sense to Brian, and it was only getting murkier. And if this Sean person was supposedly dead, who was it that he had seen walking into the Crystal Penguin on Friday?

"So where is this Sean?" he asked, struggling with a wave of angry confusion that was totally foreign to him. "Did Mom and Dad decide they could only afford to keep three of us and made us draw straws to see who'd stay and who'd go? And why haven't I heard anything about this before?"

Andrew chose his words very carefully. "Because Sean died before he was a year old." He backtracked a little to give Brian a more concise picture. "He was born between Mike and you." Andrew closed his eyes, remembering the anguish on his mother's face. Everything about the day had left an indelible impression on his young mind. "One morning, Mom got up all sunny because Sean had slept through the night for the first time. She went into the nursery to get him and then I heard her start screaming." As he spoke, it all came back to him in vivid color. "I remember Dad rushing in and then coming out with the baby in his arms, trying desperately to revive him. But it was too late to save him. He was blue. Sean'd died somewhere in the middle of the night." He felt Rose tighten her grasp on his hand. "They called it crib death back then."

"SIDS," Rose murmured. "Sudden infant death syndrome."

Andrew nodded. He noted that Brian still looked confused, and unconvinced.

"So this is what?" Brian pressed. "Sean's ghost walking the earth?"

"No," Andrew answered patiently. "But when she first brought Sean home from the hospital, I'd see Mom staring at him, shaking her head. Saying that she felt there'd been a mix-up in the hospital. That this baby didn't *feel* like *her* baby." He took a deep breath. "After Sean died, Dad told me that maybe some inherent, unconscious defense mechanism had made Mom find reasons not to get close to Sean. He said it was as if she'd subconsciously known that Sean wasn't going to live long.

"The very thought of losing Sean upset her so much, Dad told everyone at the time, including me, that we weren't to talk about Sean anymore." He looked at his youngest brother. "You were born less than a year after that. She went a little overboard and completely doted on you," he reminded Brian.

Brian shrugged, trying to lighten the moment for both his brother and himself. "I always thought it was because I was so adorable."

Andrew laughed shortly and snorted. "Not damn likely."

"So now what?" Rose prodded gently, looking from her husband to her brother-in-law and back again.

"Now," Andrew answered, "we go and find out who this guy who looks like me is—"

"And more important, exactly where and when he was born," Brian interjected. "That includes the name of the hospital."

Rose sighed. Shaking her head, she rose from the stool. "I've got a very strong feeling that I'm going to have to be buying more dishes soon." She looked at the table in the next room. "Not to mention more chairs."

Andrew laughed and gave her a one-arm hug while planting a quick kiss against her temple. "This is one of the reasons why I love you so much, Rose. You're always one step ahead of me."

"Only to keep from being trampled by the Cavanaugh brothers," she quipped just before she left the kitchen.

Since Andrew had dropped this bombshell on his unsuspecting brother, he knew that his wife had made a graceful exit so the two could talk in private. However, he had no doubt that she would ask her own questions later.

With almost five hours of sleep under her belt, Kansas was back at the shelter. Bypassing the yellow crime-scene tape that encircled the entire outer perimeter of what was left of the building, she made her way inside. Once there she began sifting through the rubble in an effort to piece together as much information as she could about what had gone on here less than a day ago.

She'd managed to find the fire's point of origin and also to rule out that the fire had been an accident. She discovered what was left of the incendiary device. It had a timer on it, which could only mean that the fire had been deliberately set, and whoever had done it had a definite time in mind. To kill someone specific? she wondered. If so, whoever had set it had miscalculated. No one had died last night.

The device wasn't a match for the MO of any of the known arsonists or pyromaniacs in the area. There was an outside chance that it could still be the work of someone belonging to one group or the other, someone who had managed to go undetected.

Until now.

It was frustrating, she thought. There *had* to be some kind of a connection, no matter how minor, if she was to believe that these weren't just random fires haphazardly set. But what connection? And why? Why these structures and not the ones down the block or somewhere else? What did these particular buildings that had been torched have in common—assuming, of course, that they actually *had* something in common?

Rocking back on her heels, Kansas ran her hand through her hair and sighed. It was like banging her head against a concrete wall. There were no answers to be found here.

"Penny for your thoughts."

Caught completely off guard, Kansas swallowed a gasp as she jumped to her feet. When she swung around, she found O'Brien watching her from a few feet away. She's been so preoccupied, she hadn't heard anyone come in. She was going to have to work on that, she told herself.

"A penny?" Kansas hooted. "Is that all it's worth to you? I take it I'm in the presence of the last of the big-time spenders."

"I don't believe in throwing my money away," he told her matter-of-factly. "I also didn't expect to find you here."

"Oh?" She looked at him, perplexed. "Tell me, just where would you expect to find a fire investigator, Detective?"

He shrugged, joining her. He looked down at the

rubble she'd been sifting through. "I just thought you'd gotten everything you needed last night."

Maybe he was a little slow on the uptake, she thought. The good-looking ones usually were.

"If I had," she pointed out patiently, crouching down again, "I'd know who did it. Or at least why. Right now, I'm still trying to find all the pieces of that puzzle," she said under her breath.

Crouching down beside her, Ethan looked at what she was doing with interest. "Find anything new?"

Amusement curved her mouth as she glanced up for a moment. "Are you asking me to do your work for you, Detective?"

"No, I'm asking you to share," he corrected. He thought the point of all this was to find who was responsible, not participate in a competition. "We're both part of the same team."

He *couldn't* be that naive. "Detective, not even different divisions of the same department are on the same team, and in case you haven't noticed, you're with the police department and I belong to the fire department. Big difference," she concluded.

He followed her statement to its logical conclusion. "So to you, this is a competition?" He wouldn't have thought that of her, but then, he reminded himself, he really didn't know this woman. Chemistry—and there was plenty of that—was not a substitute for knowledge.

It wasn't a matter of competition, Kansas thought defensively, it was a matter of sharing information with someone she trusted. Right now, she had no basis for that. Moreover, she didn't trust this man any further than she could throw him.

"To me, Detective, you're basically a stranger—"

He finished the statement for her. "And your mother taught you never to speak to strangers, right?"

One would think, after all these years, the word *mother* wouldn't create such a feeling of emptiness and loss within her. But it did.

"I'm sure she would have if I'd had one," Kansas answered, her voice distant. He looked as if he was going to say something apologetic, so she quickly went on. "What I'm saying is that you're an unknown quantity and I haven't got time to waste, wondering if you have some kind of ulterior motive...or if I can confide in you because you're really one of those pure-hearted souls who believes in truth, justice and the American way."

"I think a red cape and blue tights would go with that," he responded dryly. "Me, I'm not that noble. I just want to put this son of a bitch away before he hurts someone else—and if I have to work with the devil or share the stage with him to do it, I will."

There was only one conclusion to be drawn from that. For the second time, Kansas rose to her feet, her hands on her hips. "So now I'm the devil?" she demanded.

He looked surprised that she would come to that conclusion. "No, I didn't say that. You really are something," he freely admitted, "but *devil* isn't the word that readily comes to mind when thinking of you." He flashed a grin at her that shimmied up and down her spine and was totally out of place here. "I was just trying to let you know how far I'd be willing to go to catch this guy if I had to."

His grin, she caught herself thinking, had turned utterly sexy. And he undoubtedly knew that. She'd never met a handsome man who was unaware of the kind of charisma he wielded.

"So," Ethan was saying, "why don't we pool our resources and see what we can accomplish together? Bring your team over to the precinct," he encouraged.

It pained her to admit what she was about to say. "I *am* the team."

"Then you won't need to find a large car to drive over." Ethan put his hand out to seal the bargain. "What do you say?"

She looked down at the hand he held out to her. While she preferred working on her own, the point here was to catch whoever was setting these fires and keep him—or possibly her—from doing it again. The firebug needed to be caught as quickly as possible…before actual lives were lost.

She slipped her hand into his and shook it firmly. "Okay."

"Attagirl." He saw a look come into her eyes he couldn't fathom. Had she just taken that in a condescending manner? "Sorry, I didn't mean it the way it might have sounded. Just expressing relief that I got you to come around so quickly."

Okay, she needed to set him straight right from the beginning. "You didn't get me to 'come around so quickly,' Detective. It's just common sense. You have an entire task force devoted to tracking down this firebug." There was a safe expression, she thought. It didn't espouse any particular theory other than this unbalanced person felt a kinship to flames. "That means you have more resources available to you than I do. We can hopefully move forward more quickly and put an end to this sick reign of fire before someone *is* actually killed."

Ethan nodded in agreement. "A woman after my own heart."

She paused to pin him with a look that spoke volumes. Mostly it issued a warning. "Not even in your wildest dreams, Detective."

Ethan smiled to himself. Nothing goaded him on like a challenge. Maybe, he thought, he'd get this strong-principled, "get the hell out of my way" woman to eat her words. He had a feeling that she could be a hell of a wildcat in bed.

"If you're through here," he said, "you're welcome to come back to the precinct with me now and take a look at the information we've got."

It was probably more than she had compiled. They had only recently been entertaining the idea that the fires were connected and the work of just one person or possibly one team.

Kansas nodded. "Okay, I just might take you up on that, Detective."

"I do have a first name, you know."

Kansas looked at him with the most innocent expression she could muster. "You mean it's not 'Detective'?"

"It's Ethan."

Like he was telling her something she didn't already know. She made it a point to access all the information she could about the people whose paths she crossed.

"Yes, I know. What floor are you on, Detective?" She deliberately used his title.

Ethan laughed softly under his breath. She'd come around in her own time. And if she didn't, well, he could live with that. She wasn't the last beautiful woman he'd ever encounter.

"Third," he answered. "Why?"

She packed up some of the tools she'd been using to collect evidence. "Well, here's a wild thought—so I know where I'm going."

He looked at her quizzically. "I thought I'd take you."

"Yes, I know," she told him. "I'd rather take myself if it's all the same to you. Besides, there's something I need to do first before going to the precinct."

He made an educated guess as to what that was. "You don't have to run this past your captain. The chief of D's has already cleared it with him."

She didn't like being second-guessed. It made her feel hemmed in. "That's all well and good, but that's not what I need to do first."

She still wasn't elaborating. "You always this vague about things?" he wondered.

Her smile widened. "Keeps people guessing." *And me safe,* she added silently. Slipping the recorder she'd been using to tape her thoughts into her case, she snapped the locks into place and picked up the case. "I'll see you in a bit."

He had no idea if she intended to make good on that or if she was just saying it to humor him. All he knew was that he fully intended to see her again, fire or no fire.

* * *

Dax paced back and forth before the bulletin boards in the front of the room.

"There's *got* to be some kind of pattern here," he insisted, staring at the three bulletin boards he'd had brought into the task force's makeshift squad room.

Each fire had its own column with as much information as they could find listed directly beneath it. All the fires had all broken out in the last six months in and around Aurora. Other than that, there was nothing uniform and no attention-grabbing similarities about them.

And yet, he had a gut feeling that there had to be. What was he missing?

"If there is," Ortiz commented in a lackluster tone, "I can't see it." Rocking in his seat, Ortiz slowly sipped his extra-large container of chai tea. He drank the beverage religiously at least once a day, claiming it gave him mental clarity.

The others knew better. Especially after Ethan had pointed out that Ortiz liked to flirt with the cute dark-haired girl behind the counter who filled the detective's order as well as his less-than-anemic imagination.

"Maybe we're including too many fires," Ethan speculated, gesturing at the bulletin boards with its news clippings.

"Isn't that the point?" Youngman questioned. "These are all the fires that've taken place in and around Aurora in the last six months. If we don't include all of them, we might come up with the *wrong* pattern."

He knew he was playing devil's advocate here, but they had to explore all the avenues before they found the one that would lead them to the right answer. To the man or men responsible for all that destruction.

"But maybe they weren't all set by the same guy," Ethan insisted.

"But they *were* all set."

Ethan, Dax, Youngman and Ortiz all turned to see Kansas walking into the small, cluttered room that the task force was temporarily using to cut down on any distractions from the other detectives.

She walked as if she owned the room.

"And we won't come up with the wrong answer," she assured them with feeling. "If we just keep talking all this out long enough, we're going to either find the answer, which has been right in front of us all along, or stumble across something that'll eventually lead us to the right answer.

"But one way or the other," Kansas concluded, "we *are* going to get to the bottom of this."

Her eyes swept over the four detectives. There was no mistaking the confidence in her voice.

Ethan couldn't help wondering if she meant it, or if she was just saying that for their benefit, giving them a glimpse of her own version of whistling in the dark to keep the demons at bay.

It wouldn't be the first time that he'd encountered female bravado. Because of his sister, Greer, he'd been raised with it. He had a gut feeling that the two women were very much alike.

# Chapter 6

Ethan was the first to break the silence.

"My money's still on an arsonist doing this," he said even though he knew that the new, adjunct member of the team vehemently disagreed with this theory.

Kansas thought about holding her tongue. She was, after all, the outsider here, and arguing was not the way to become part of the team. She'd stated her point of view and should just let it go at that.

But she'd never been one to merely go with the flow. It just wasn't part of her nature. The words seemed to come out almost of their own accord.

"Where's the profit to be gained from burning down a church and an abused-women's shelter that's already pretty run-down?" she challenged.

"Real estate," Ethan argued. "The places aren't worth anything as they are, and there might be little or no insurance on the structures, so there's definitely not enough money to rebuild. That would make whoever owns the property willing and maybe eager to sell." He shrugged. "Maybe they feel that they can start somewhere else with the money they get from selling the land the property stands on."

Kansas rolled her eyes at his explanation. "So, in your opinion, some big, bad CEO is paying someone to run around and burn down buildings in and around Aurora in order to put together a colossal shopping mall or something to that effect?"

Ethan scowled. He didn't care for her dismissive tone. "It sounds stupid when you say it that way," he accused.

"That's because it *is* stupid—no matter which way you say it," Kansas pointed out, happy that he got the point.

Dax literally got in between his cousin and the woman his father felt they needed to work with.

"Children, children, play nice," he instructed, looking from one to the other to make sure that his words sank in. "And in the meantime," he said, turning to another detective, "Ortiz, see if you can check with Records down at the civic center to see if anyone has put in for permits to start building anything of any consequence."

"If Ortiz doesn't find anything, it doesn't mean the theory doesn't hold up," Ethan interjected.

Dax crossed his arms before his chest, striking a pose that said he was waiting for more. "Go ahead. I'm listening."

"It just means that whoever it is who's doing this hasn't had time to properly file his intent to build whatever it is that he's going to build," Ethan explained. "The destroyed properties are far from desirable, so maybe he figures he has time. And the longer he takes to get to 'step two,' the less likely it'll be that someone will make the connection between the arson and the motive behind it."

Kansas supposed that O'Brien had a point. She wasn't so married to her theory that she would stubbornly shut her eyes to exclude everything else.

"Maybe we should check out whether anyone's bought any of the properties previously destroyed by the fires," she suggested.

"Then you're on board with this theory?" O'Brien asked. There was a touch of triumph in his voice that irritated her. It had her reverting to her original theory.

"No, I just want to put it to rest once and for all." Her eyes narrowed ever so slightly as she continued. "I'd stake my job that this isn't a fire-for-hire situation." She could feel it in her bones, but she wasn't about to say that out loud. She didn't know these people well enough to allow them to laugh at her, even good-naturedly. "It's some pyromaniac getting his high out of watching everyone scramble, trying to keep the fire from destroying another piece of real estate. Another person's hopes and dreams."

Dax was still open to all possibilities until something started to gel. "Okay, why don't you and Youngman go check it out," he instructed her. "Begin with the first fire on the list and work your way up."

But Youngman shook his head. "No can do, Dax. I've got that dental appointment to go to. Doc says it's going to take the better part of two hours to do the root canal." He cupped his right cheek to underscore his situation. "I'd cancel, but I already did that once, and this thing is just *killing* me."

Dax nodded. Youngman had already told him about the appointment this morning. Things were getting so hectic, he'd just forgotten. "Go. Get it seen to." Without missing a beat, Dax turned to his cousin. "Take his place, Ethan."

"In the dental chair?" Ethan asked hopefully.

"Very funny. You, her, go," Dax said, nodding toward the door. "See what you can come up with that might get your theory to float."

"An anchor comes to mind," Kansas muttered under her breath.

Grabbing his jacket and slipping it on, Ethan shot her an annoyed look. He was going to enjoy putting her in her place. And then, once the shrew was tamed, other possibilities might open up, he mused.

"I'll drive," he announced as they left the squad room. He punched the down button for the elevator.

The statement was met with a careless shrug. "If it's that important to you, I wouldn't dream of fighting with you about it," she murmured.

The elevator car arrived and she stepped in. He was quick to get in with her, then pressed the button for the first floor.

"It's not important to me," he informed her, his irritation growing. Supposedly, the woman was agreeing with him. But it was the manner in which she was agreeing that he found annoying. "It's just that—"

She turned the most innocent expression he'd ever seen in his direction. "Yes?"

The woman was playing him. The second the steel doors parted, he all but shot out of the elevator, heading for the precinct entrance. "Never mind," he ground out. "You want to drive? Because if you do, we'll take your car."

She preceded him outside. There was a soft spring breeze rustling through everything, quietly reminding them that at any moment, it could pick up and fan any flames it encountered.

"You don't trust me with your car?" she asked. *Typical male*, she thought.

"I don't trust *anybody* with my car," he told her. "I spent too much time, effort and money restoring her to just hand the keys over to someone else."

Sounded like the man was obsessed with his car, she thought. The smile she raised to her lips was the embodiment of serenity. "You can drive," she told him. "It's okay."

She was yanking his chain—and a few other things, as well. He led the way to his car, parked over in the third row. "Why do I get the feeling that you're laughing at me?"

The woman looked as if she were seriously considering the question. "My first guess would be insecurity," she said brightly.

"Your first guess would be wrong," he retorted.

She paused before the cream-colored two-seater. She wasn't really up on cars, but she recognized it as a classic. "It really is a beauty," she told him.

The compliment instantly softened him. "Thanks."

He pressed the security button on his key chain and released the locks. "You have the list of sites where the fires took place?" he asked. Since she'd already gotten in on her side, he slid in behind the steering wheel—and saw that instead of buckling up, she was holding up several sheets of paper. He presumed they were the list he'd referred to. "Okay, where to first?"

"How about MacArthur and Main?" she suggested after a beat. "That's the church," she explained, shifting as she buckled her seat belt. "That was the second fire," she added in case he'd forgotten.

He hadn't. "Where that firefighter rescued the visiting priest from Spain. The priest was sleeping in Father Colm's room," he recalled.

She vividly remembered all the details of that one. Daring, last-minute rescues like that always tugged on her heartstrings. "There was footage of the old priest being carried out of the burning building."

The media, always hungry for something to sink its teeth into, carried the story for days, and the morning talk shows vied for the exclusive rights to being the first to interview both the firefighter and the priest, sitting in the studio side by side.

He thought of the theory that he'd espoused. It seemed rather shaky here. "I really doubt that the church is being put up for sale."

"I doubt it, too," she agreed. Since he'd backed off, she could afford to be magnanimous. "But we can still ask if anyone made any offers on the property since the fire." She shrugged again. "At any rate, it's better than nothing."

As he drove, he slanted a glance at her, looking for

confirmation in her expression. "You're humoring me, aren't you?"

"No," she said honestly, sitting back in her seat, "what I'm trying to do is prove or disprove your theory once and for all so we can move on."

He knew which side of the argument she was on, and he didn't care for being summarily dismissed. "What if it turns out that I'm right?"

"Then, most likely," she recited, "you'll be impossible to live with and I'll be happy that I'm not part of the police department, because I won't have to put up with it. But even if hell does freeze over and you're right, the upshot will be that we've caught the person or persons responsible for all this destruction, and that'll be a very good thing." And then the corners of her mouth curved in a forced smile. "But you won't be right, so there's no point in anticipating it."

The woman was being downright smug, he thought. Since when did he find smug so arousing? "You're that sure?"

She lifted her chin ever so slightly, making it a good target, he couldn't help thinking. Damn, his feelings were bouncing all over the place today. "I'm that sure."

The light up ahead turned yellow. In any other car he would have stepped on the gas and flown through. But this was his baby, and he eased into a stop at the intersection several beats before the light turned red.

"Tell me," he said, turning toward her, "do you walk on water all the time, or just on Sundays?"

"Mainly Sundays," she answered with a straight face. There wasn't even a hint of a smile. "There's the church." She pointed to the building in the distance on the right. "Looks like it's being rebuilt."

The light turned green. Ethan drove over to the church and said nothing as he pulled the vehicle into the parking lot. He brought his vehicle to a stop in front of the partially demolished building.

Kansas was out of the car before he had a chance to pull up the handbrake. For a woman who was wearing rather high heels, she moved inordinately quickly, he thought.

Kansas was more than several strides ahead of him by the time he got out.

"Father," she called out to the cleric, waving her hand to get his attention.

A white-haired man in jeans and a sweatshirt, its sleeves pushed all the way back beyond his elbows, turned around in response to her call. He was holding on to the base of a ladder that was up against the side of the church, keeping it steady while a much younger man stood close to the top, trying to spread an even layer of stucco.

Kansas flipped her wallet open to her ID and held it up for the priest to see as she approached. "I'm Investigator Kansas Beckett—with the fire department." Putting her ID away, she nodded toward Ethan. "This is Detective Ethan O'Brien with the Aurora PD. We're looking into this awful fire that almost took down your church, Father."

"*Almost* being the key word," the priest responded with a pleased smile. He turned back to look at the church. His smile told her that he was seeing beyond what was currently standing before them.

"I see that you're rebuilding," Ethan observed.

"Not me," the priest answered modestly. "I'm just holding the ladder, stirring paint, that sort of thing. St. Angela's is blessed to have such a talented congregation." He beamed, looking up the ladder he was holding steady. "Mr. Wicks is a general contractor who, luckily for us, is temporarily in between assignments, and he kindly volunteered to give us the benefit of his expertise."

The man Father Colm was referring to climbed down the ladder. Once his feet were on the ground, he shook hands with Ethan and Kansas, holding on to her hand, she noted, a beat longer than necessary. But she did like the appreciative smile on his lips as he looked at her.

Flattery without any possibility of entanglement. The best of all worlds, she thought.

"By 'in between,' Father Colm means unemployed." Wicks regarded the older man with affection. "I'm just glad to help. It keeps me active and allows me to practice my trade so I don't forget what to do. It's been a *long* dry spell," he confessed.

"With so many of the parishioners volunteering their time and talent, it won't be long before we have the church whole and functional again," the priest informed them with no small amount of pride.

It was as good an opening as any, Kansas thought. "Father, right after the fire—"

"Terrible, terrible time," the priest murmured, shaking his head. His bright blue eyes shone with tears as he recalled. "I was afraid that the Vatican wouldn't approve of our being here any longer and would just authorize everyone to attend Our Lady of Angels Church on the other end of Aurora."

Kansas waited politely for the priest to finish unloading the sentiments that were weighing down on him. When he stopped, she continued her line of questioning. "Did anyone come with an offer to take the property off your hands? Or, more aptly I guess, off the Church's hands?"

"The only ones who approached me," Father Colm told her and O'Brien, "were Mr. Wick and some of the other parishioners. Everyone's been so generous, donating either their time, or money, or sometimes even both, to rebuild St. Angela's." He sighed deeply. "I am a very, very blessed man." There was a hitch in his voice and he stopped to clear it.

Ethan rephrased the question, asking it again, just to be perfectly clear about the events. "So, you're sure that no one offered to give you money for the property, saying you'd be better off starting over somewhere else from the ground up?"

"No, Detective O'Brien," the priest assured him. "I might be old, but I would have remembered that. Because I would have said no. I've been here for thirty-six years. I'm too old to start at a new location." And then he paused, looking from one to the other, before exchanging puzzled looks with the general contractor. "Why do you ask?"

O'Brien hesitated. Kansas saw no reason for secrecy, not with the priest. So she was the one who answered the man. "We're investigating the rash of recent fires in Aurora. Yours was among the first. We're attempting to find a common motive."

Father Colm looked horrified. "You seriously think

that someone *deliberately* tried to burn down St. Angela's?"

"All evidence points to the fact that the fire here wasn't just an accident. It was set," Ethan told the priest.

"You're kidding," Wicks said, looking as if he'd been broadsided.

Father Colm shook his head, his expression adamant. "No, I refuse to think of this as a hate crime, Detective O'Brien. That's just too terrible a thought to entertain."

"I don't believe that it was a hate crime, either," Kansas assured him. Although, she supposed that would be another avenue they could explore if they ran out of options. "This is the only church that was burned down. If it were a hate crime, there would have been at least a few more places of worship, more churches targeted. Instead, the range of structures that were torched is quite wide and diverse."

The priest looked as if he were struggling to absorb the theory. "But the fires were all deliberately set?"

O'Brien looked as if he were searching for a diplomatic way to phrase his answer. Kansas took the straightforward path. "Yes."

The old man, a priest for fifty-one years, appeared shell-shocked. "Why?" The question came out in a hoarse whisper.

"That, Father, is what we're trying to find out," Ethan told him, thinking that they had just come full circle. He was quick to launch into basic questions of his own.

Again the priest, and this time Wicks, were asked if there was anything unusual about that day, anything out of the ordinary that either of them could remember seeing or hearing, no matter how minor.

Nothing came to either of the men's minds.

Kansas nodded. She really hadn't expected any earthshaking revelations. Hoped, but hadn't expected.

She dug into her pocket and retrieved two of her cards. "If either of you *do* think of anything," Kansas told the men as she held out her business cards, offering one to each of them, "please call me."

Ethan gave the priest and Wicks his own card. "Please call us," he amended, glancing in Kansas's direction and silently reprimanding her for what he took to be her attempt to edge him out.

"Right, us," Kansas corrected with a quirk of a smile that came and left her lips in less than a heartbeat. "I forgot I'm temporarily assigned to Detective O'Brien's task force," she confided to the priest.

Father Colm nodded, apparently giving his whole-hearted approval to the venture. "The more minds working on this, the faster this terrible situation will be resolved."

She'd never gone to any house of worship. There'd been no one to urge her to choose one religion over the other, no one to care if she prayed or not. But if she were to choose a single place, she thought, it would be one whose pastor was loving and kind. A pastor like Father Colm.

Kansas flashed a grin at the cleric. "From your lips to God's ears," she said, reciting a phrase she'd once heard one of the social workers say to one of the other children in the group home.

Father Colm laughed warmly in response. Kansas

found the sound strangely reassuring. "I'll be back," she promised.

The bright blue eyes met hers. "Feel free to stop by anytime," the priest urged. "God's house is always open to you."

Kansas merely nodded as she left.

O'Brien and she made no headway of any kind at site of the second fire. The charred remains of the building were still there, abandoned by one and all and presently neglected by the city. Kansas made a mental note to look up the current status of the property and see who owned it.

The site of the third fire, a movie triplex that had gone up in flames long after the last show had let out, appeared to be suffering the same fate as the second site. Except that someone had put in a bid for it.

In front of the burnt-out shell that had once contained three movie theaters was a relatively new sign announcing that several stores were coming soon to that area. The name of the developer was printed in block letters on the bottom right-hand side of the sign. Brad McCormack and Sons.

Kansas wrote the name down in her small, battered notepad. "What do you say to paying Mr. McCormack a visit?" she asked when she finished.

"Sure," Ethan agreed. He glanced at his watch. "How about right after lunch?"

"It's too early for lunch," she protested. She wanted to keep going until they actually had something to work with.

"It's almost noon," he pointed out. "What time do you eat lunch?"

It couldn't be that late. Kansas glanced at her watch, ready to prove him wrong. Except that she couldn't. "You're right," she muttered.

"I know. I had to learn how to tell time before they'd let me join the police force," he told her dryly.

She sighed, walking back to his car. "Did you have to learn sarcasm, as well? Or was that something you brought to the table on your own?"

"The latter." He waited until she got in. Because she'd leaned her hand on the car's hood for a moment, Ethan doubled back and wiped way the print with a handkerchief before finally getting in on his side. He didn't have to look at her to know that Kansas had rolled her eyes. "And speaking of table, where would you like to go for lunch?"

He wasn't going to stop until she gave in, she thought. That could start a dangerous precedent. *Where the hell had that come from?* she wondered, caught off guard by her own thoughts.

Out loud she asked, "What is it with you and food?"

"I like having it. Keeps me from being grumpy." He looked at her pointedly as he started up the vehicle. "You might want to think about trying it sometime. Might do wonders for your personality."

She let the comment pass. "All right, since you have to eat, how about a drive-through?"

He was thinking more in terms of sitting back and recharging for an hour. "How about a sit-down restaurant with table and chairs?" he countered.

She merely looked at him. "Takes less than twenty minutes to start a fire."

*Yeah,* he thought, his eyes washing over the woman sitting next to him in the vehicle. *Tell me something I didn't already know.*

And then he sighed. "Drive-through it is."

## Chapter 7

"Is it okay to pull over somewhere and eat this, or do we have to ingest lunch while en route to the next destination?" Ethan asked dryly, driving away from the fast-food restaurant's take-out window.

The bag with their lunches was resting precariously against his thigh while the two containers of economy-sized sodas were nestled in the vehicle's cup holders. The plastic lids that covered the containers looked far from secure.

Amused rather than annoyed by the detective's sarcasm, Kansas answered, "It's okay to pull over. I just meant that going inside a restaurant is usually a full-hour proposition, especially at this time of day. And if we're going to spend time together, I'd rather it was at one of the sites where the fires took place."

Driving to a relatively empty corner of the parking lot that accommodated seven different fast-food establishments, Ethan pulled up the parking brake. He rolled down his window and shut off the engine. Glancing inside the oversized paper bag he'd been awarded at the drive-through window, he pulled out a long, tubular, green-wrapped item and held it out to her.

"This is yours, I believe. I ordered the cheese-burger."

"I know. Not exactly very imaginative," Kansas commented, taking the meat-and-cheese wrap from him.

She tried not to notice how infectious his grin was. "Sue me. I like basic things. I'm a very uncomplicated guy."

*Uncomplicated?* Kansas raised her eyes to his. *Who does he think he's kidding?*

Drop-dead gorgeous men with their own agendas were generally as difficult to figure out as a Rubik's Cube. Definitely *not* uncomplicated.

"Yeah, I'll bet," she muttered audibly just before taking her first bite.

With a cheeseburger in one hand, he reached into the bag with the other and pulled out several French fries. He held them out to her. "Want some of my fries?" he offered.

She shook her head, swallowing another bite. She hadn't realized until she'd started eating just how hungry she actually was. If she didn't know better, she would have said her stomach was celebrating. "No, I'm good, thanks."

A hint of a smile curved his mouth. "I'm sure you are."

The low, sultry tone he'd used had her looking at him again, but she kept silent. She had a feeling that she was better off not knowing the explanation behind his words. No doubt, the path to seduction, or what he perceived as the path to seduction, was mixed in there somewhere.

Giving her full attention to eating the turkey-and-pastrami wrap she'd ordered, Kansas was in no way prepared for what came next.

"You never knew your mother?"

The bite she'd just taken went down her windpipe instead of her esophagus. She started coughing until there were tears in her eyes. Abandoning his lunch, Ethan twisted her in her seat and began pounding on her back until she held her hand up in surrender.

"It's okay. I'm okay," she protested, trying to catch her breath. When she finally did, her eyes still somewhat watery, she looked at O'Brien. "Where did that come from?"

He slid back into his seat. "From what you said earlier."

Her mind a blank, she shook her head. "I don't recall."

He had a feeling that she remembered but was dismissing the subject outright. "When I made that crack about your mother teaching you not to talk to strangers and you answered that you were sure she would have if you'd had one."

Kansas placed what was left of the wrap down on the paper it had come in and looked at him. "Where is this going?"

There was a dangerous note in her voice that warned

him to tread lightly. Or better yet, back off. "I was just curious if your mother died when you were very young."

Her expression was stony as she told him, "I have no idea if she's dead or alive. Now could we drop this?" she asked in the coldest tone she'd ever summoned.

It wasn't cold enough. "You didn't know her." It didn't take much of a stretch for him to guess that.

The first reply that came to her lips was to tell him to damn well mind his own business, but she had a feeling that the retort would fall on deaf ears. He didn't strike her as the type to back off unless he wanted to. The best way to be done with this was just to answer his question as directly and precisely as possible.

"No, I didn't know her." She addressed her answer to the windshield as she stared straight ahead. "All I know is that she left me on the steps of a hospital when I was a few days old."

Sympathy and pity as well as a wave of empathy stirred within him. There'd been times, when he was much younger, when he'd felt the sting of missing a parent, but his mother had always been there for all of them. What must it have been like for her, not having either in her life?

"You're an orphan?"

He saw her jawline harden. "That's one of the terms for it. 'Throwaway' was another one someone once used," she recalled, her voice distant, devoid of any feeling.

She wasn't fooling him. Something like that came wrapped in pain that lasted a lifetime. "No one ever adopted you?"

She finally turned toward him. Her mouth quirked in a smile that didn't reach her eyes. "Hard to believe that no one wanted me, seeing as how I have this sweet personality and all?" One of the social workers had called her unadoptable after a third set of foster parents had brought her back.

He knew what she was doing, and he hadn't meant to make her feel self-conscious or bring back any painful memories. "I'm sorry."

Her back was up even as she carelessly shrugged away his apology. "Hey, things happen."

"Do you ever wonder—"

She knew what he was going to ask. If she ever wondered about who her parents had been. Or maybe if she wondered what it would have been like if at least her mother had kept her. She had, in both cases, but she wasn't about to talk to him about it. That was something she kept locked away.

"No," she said sharply, cutting him off. "Never." Balling up the remainder of her lunch, she tossed it and the wrapper into the bag. "Now, unless you've secretly been commissioned to write my biography, I'd appreciate it if you'd stop asking me questions that aren't going to further this investigation." She nodded at the burger he was still holding. "Finish your lunch."

Not until he evened the playing field for her, he thought. He didn't want her thinking he was trying to be superior or put her down in any manner. That was not the way he operated.

"I never knew my father."

Oh no, they weren't going to sit here, swapping deep-down secrets that he hoped would ultimately disarm her so that he could get into her bed. It wasn't going to work that way. It had once, but she'd been very young and vulnerable then. And stupid. She'd grown up a lot since she'd made that awful mistake and married a man she thought could be her shelter from the cruelties of life. Grown up enough to know that there would never be anyone out there to love her the way she needed to be loved.

The way she so desperately wanted to be loved.

Like it or not, she'd made her peace with that and she wasn't about to suddenly grow stupid because the guy sitting across from her with the chiseled profile and the soulfully beautiful blue eyes was doing his best to sound "nice."

Kansas looked at him and said flatly, "I don't want to know this."

Ethan didn't seem to hear her. Or, if he did, it didn't deter him. He went on as if she hadn't said anything.

"My mother told us he died on the battlefield, saving his friends. That he was a hero." For a moment, a faraway look came into his eyes as bits and pieces of that time came back to him. "She told us a lot of things about our father, always emphasizing that we had a lot to be proud of."

She had no idea why he was telling her this. Did he think that sharing this was going to somehow bring them closer? "Okay, so you had a legend for a father and I didn't. How does this—"

She didn't get to finish framing her question. His eyes met hers and he said very simply, without emotion, "She lied."

That brought what she was about to say to a screeching halt. Kansas stared at him. "Excuse me?"

"She lied," he repeated and then, for emphasis, said again, "My mother lied."

Despite her initial resolve, Kansas could feel herself being drawn in ever so slowly. It was the look in his eyes that did it. She supposed, since O'Brien seemed so bent on talking, that she might as well try to gain a measure of control over the conversation. "About his being a hero?"

*If only,* Ethan thought. If it had just been that, he could have easily made his peace with it. But it went far beyond a mere white lie. And it made him slow to trust anyone other than Kyle and Greer, the only two people in the world who had been as affected as him by this revelation.

"About all of it. Everything she'd told us was just a lie."

Kansas felt for him. She would have been devastated in his place. *If* what he said was true. "How did you find out?"

"From her. On her deathbed." *God, that sounded so melodramatic,* he thought. But it was the truth. Had his mother not been dying, he was certain that the lie would have continued indefinitely. "She knew she didn't have much longer, and apparently she wanted to die with a clear conscience."

Kansas took a guess as to what was behind the initial lie. "She didn't know who your father was?"

"Oh, she knew, all right." An edge entered Ethan's voice. "He was the man who abandoned her when she told him she was pregnant. The man who bullied her into not telling anyone about the relationship they'd had. If she did, according to what she told us, he promised that he would make her life a living hell."

Kansas didn't know what to say. Going by her own feelings in this sort of a situation, she instinctively knew he wouldn't want her pity. She shook her head, commiserating. "Sounds like a winner."

"Yeah, well, not every Cavanaugh turned out to be sterling—although, so far, my 'father' seems to be the only one in the family who dropped the ball."

The last name made her sit up and take notice. Her eyes widened. "Are you telling me that Brian Cavanaugh is your father?"

He realized that he hadn't been specific. "No, it's not Brian—"

"Andrew?" she interjected. She'd never met the man, but the detective had mentioned him and she knew the man by reputation. The very thought that Andrew Cavanaugh would have a love child he refused to publicly acknowledge sounded completely preposterous, especially since he was known for throwing open his doors to *everyone*.

But then, she thought, reconsidering, did anyone really ever know anyone else? When she'd gotten married, she would have sworn that Grant would never hurt her—and she'd been incredibly wrong about that.

"No, not Andrew, either." He would have been proud to call either man his father, but life hardly ever arranged itself perfectly.

She frowned. *Was* he pulling her leg? "All the other Cavanaughs are too young," she retorted. The oldest was possibly ten or twelve years older than O'Brien. Maybe less.

"It was Mike Cavanaugh," he said flatly.

Mike. Michael. Kansas shook her head. "I'm afraid I don't know who that is."

"Was," he corrected her. "Mike Cavanaugh died in the line of duty a number of years ago. Patience and Patrick are his legitimate kids—"

She stopped him cold. He was treading on terrain that encompassed one of her pet peeves.

"Every kid is 'legitimate,'" she said with feeling. "It's the parents who aren't always legitimate, not thinking beyond the moment or weighing any of the consequences of their actions. Allowing themselves to get careless and carried away without any regard for who they might wind up hurting—"

Ethan held up his hand to get her to stop. "I'm not trying to get into an argument with you," he told her. "I'm trying to make you see that we have more in common than you think."

*Not really,* she thought.

"At least you *had* a mother, a mother who tried to shield you from her mistake, however badly she might have done it. A mother who tried to give you something to believe in. Mine couldn't be bothered to do anything except to literally pin a name on me that would always make me the butt of jokes." She saw him looking at her quizzically and elaborated. "She pinned a piece of paper to my blanket that said, 'Her name is Kansas. I can't raise her.' That's it. Eight words. My entire legacy, eight words."

"At least she did give you a chance to live," he pointed

out. "I've seen newborn babies thrown out in garbage cans, discarded by the wayside, like spoiled meat." He recalled one specific case that had taken him months to get out of his head.

Kansas sat silent in the car, studying him for a long moment. Just as the silence began to seem as if it was going on too long, she said, "You're a silver-lining kind of guy, aren't you?"

Kyle had been the last one to accuse him of that, except that the terminology his brother had used wasn't quite as squeaky-clean as what Kansas had just said.

"Once in a while," he allowed. "It does help sometimes."

Kansas didn't agree. Optimists tended to be stomped on. She'd been down that route and learned her lesson early on.

"Being a realist helps," she countered. "That way, you don't wind up being disappointed." Her mouth feeling exceptionally dry, she stopped to drain the last of her soft drink. "What do you say we get this show on the road and go talk to Mr. Silver, the owner of that discount store that burned down?" In case he'd forgotten, she prompted, "It was the fourth fire."

He nodded, recalling the notes he'd written beneath the photos on the bulletin board. "That was the fire that led the chief of D's to believe that there was just one person setting all of them."

"Right." Captain Lawrence had mentioned that to her in passing.

O'Brien turned the key in the ignition and started the car. Just as he was about to shift out of Park, she put her hand on top of his, stopping him. He could have sworn he felt something akin to electricity pass through him just then. Masking it, he looked at Kansas quizzically.

"This all stays here, right?" she questioned sharply. "What we just talked about, my background, it stays here, between us. It goes no further. Right?" This time it sounded more like an order than a question. Or, at the very least, like a sharply voiced request for a confirmation.

"Absolutely," he assured her immediately. Pulling out of the spot and then merging onto the street, he slanted a glance in her direction. "But if you find you ever want to just talk about it—"

She cut him off before he could complete his offer. "I won't."

*The lady doth protest too much,* he thought. "Okay," he allowed. "But should hell begin to freeze over and you find that you've changed your mind, you know where to find me."

"Don't worry," Kansas assured him. "I won't be looking."

She bottled things up too much, he thought. He'd had one of his friends, a firefighter at another house, discreetly ask around about this woman. She didn't go out of her way to socialize and definitely didn't hang out with the firefighters after hours. She was, for all intents and purposes, a loner. Loners tended to be lonely people, and while he had no illusions or desires to change the course of her life, he did want to offer her his friendship, for whatever that was worth to her.

"Ever heard that poem about no man being an island?" he asked.

She could feel her back going up even as she tried to tell herself that O'Brien didn't mean anything by this. That he wasn't trying to demean her.

"Yeah," she acknowledged with a dismissive tone. "It was about men. Women have a different set of rules."

He doubted that she really believed that. She was just being defensive. She did that a lot, he realized. "Underneath it all, we're just human beings."

"Stop trying to get into my head, O'Brien," she warned. "You'll find it's very inhospitable territory."

He debated letting this drop and saying nothing. The debate was short. "You're trying too hard, Kansas."

God, she hated her name. It always sounded as if the person addressing her were being sarcastic. "Excuse me?"

"I said you're trying too hard," he repeated, knowing that she'd heard him the first time. "You don't have to be so macho. This isn't strictly a man's field anymore. Trust me, just be yourself and you'll have the men around here jumping through hoops every time you crook your little finger."

Was he serious? Did he actually think she was going to fall for that? "I don't know if that's insulting me or you. Or both."

"Wasn't meant to do either," he said easily, making a right turn to the next corner. He slowed down as he did so and gave her a quick glance. "You really are a beautiful woman, you know."

She straightened, doing her best to look indignant even as a warmth insisted on spreading through her. "I'd rather be thought of as an intelligent, sharp woman, not a beautiful one."

He saw no conflict in that. "You can be both," he answered matter-of-factly, then added more softly, "You are both."

Kansas frowned. Oh, he was a charmer, this temporary partner of hers. He was probably accustomed to women dropping like flies whenever he decided to lay it on. Well, he was in for a surprise. She wasn't going to let herself believe a word coming out of his mouth, no matter how tempting that was or how guileless he sounded as he delivered those words. She'd had the infection and gotten the cure. She was never going to allow herself to be led astray again. Ever.

"Don't you know that ingesting too much sugar can lead to diabetes?" she asked sarcastically.

"I'll keep that in mind," he promised, not bothering to keep a straight face. "Were the cross streets for that discount house Culver and Bryan?"

"Culver and Trabuco," she corrected.

As soon as she said it, he remembered. "That's right." He laughed shortly. "After a while, all the names and descriptions start running together."

"Not to me," she informed him crisply. "Each and every one of the buildings are different. Like people," she added.

The way she said it, he knew she wasn't trying to sound high-handed or find fault with him. She meant it. It was almost as if every fire had a separate meaning for her.

Ethan had a feeling that the fire inspector he'd initially felt that he'd been saddled with had more than one outstanding secret in her closet. He meant to find out how many and what they were, although, for the life of him, he couldn't clearly state *why* he was so determined to do this. Why he wanted to unravel the mystery that was Kansas Beckett.

But he did.

## Chapter 8

They were getting nowhere.

Five days of diligently combing through ashes, testimonies and the arrest records of felons who had a penchant for playing with fire hadn't brought them to any new conclusions, other than to reinforce what they already knew: that there were some very strange sociopaths walking the earth.

Their lack of headway wasn't for lack of tips. What they did lack for, however, were tips that didn't take them on elaborate wild-goose chases.

With a frustrated sigh, Ethan leaned back in his chair. He rocked slightly as he stared off into space. The lack of progress was getting to him. The latest "person of interest" he was looking into turned out to have been in jail when the fire spree initially started. Which brought them back to square one.

Again.

"I'm beginning to feel like a dog chasing his own tail," he said out loud, not bothering to hide his disgust.

Kansas looked up from the computer screen she'd been reading. "I'd pay to see that," she volunteered.

Closing her eyes, Kansas passed her hand over her forehead. There was a headache building there, and she felt as if she were going cross-eyed. She'd lost track of the number of hours she'd been sitting here, at the desk that had been temporarily assigned to her, going through databases that tracked recent fires throughout the western states in hopes of finding something that might lead to the firebug's identity. Every single possibility had led to a dead end.

There had to be something they were missing, she thought in exasperation. Fires that could be traced to accelerants just didn't start themselves. Who the hell was doing this, and when was he finally going to slip up?

Noting the way Kansas was rubbing her forehead, Ethan opened his bottom drawer and dug out the container with his supply of extra-strength aspirin in it. In the interest of efficiency, he always bought the economy size. He rounded his desk and placed the container on top of hers.

The sound of pills jostling against one another as he set the bottle down had Kansas opening her eyes again. She saw the bottle, then raised her eyes to his. "What's that?"

"Modern science calls it aspirin. You can call it whatever you want," Ethan told her, sitting down at his desk again. Because she was looking at the oversized bottle as if she wasn't sure what it might really hold, he said, "You look like you have a headache. I thought a few aspirins might help."

Picking the bottle up, Kansas shook her head in wonder. "This has *got* to be the biggest supply of aspirin I've ever seen."

"We get it by the truckload around here," Dax told her as he walked into the room, catching the tail end of the conversation. He raised his voice slightly to catch the rest of the task force's attention. "I suggest you all take a few with you."

Kansas swung her chair around to face Dax. A leaden feeling descended on her chest. There could be only one reason why he was saying that. "Another one?"

"Another one," Dax confirmed grimly. "Just got the call."

Ethan was on his feet, grabbing his jacket and slipping it on. "Where?"

"Down on Sand Canyon," he answered. "The place is called Meadow Hills."

Kansas stopped dead. She recognized the name instantly. "That's a nursing home," she said to Dax, but even as she said it, she was hoping that somehow she was wrong.

She wasn't.

Dax nodded, holding a tight rein on his thoughts. He was not about to let his imagination run away with him. "Yeah."

Kansas shuddered, trying to curtail the wave of horror that washed over her. She couldn't get the image of terrified senior citizens out of her head.

"What a monster," she muttered.

"It's still in progress," Dax told them as they all

hurried out the door. "Luckily, the firefighters got there quickly again. They've been a regular godsend. They had a lot of people to clear out, and I'd hate to think of what might have happened if they'd delayed their response even by a few minutes."

Kansas said nothing. She didn't even want to think about it, about how helpless and frightened some of those older residents of the convalescent home had to feel, their bodies immobilized in beds as they smelled smoke and then having that smoke fill their fragile lungs.

Another wave of frustration assaulted her, intensifying the pain in her head.

"Why can't we find this bastard?" she cried, directing the question more to herself than to any of the men who were hurrying down the hall along with her.

"Because he's good," Ethan answered plainly. "He's damn good."

"But he's not perfect," she shot back angrily.

"That's what we're all counting on," Dax told her.

Reaching the elevator first, Kansas jabbed the down button. When it failed to arrive immediately, she turned on her heel and hurried over to the door that led to the stairwell.

Ethan was quick to follow her. "Running down the stairs really isn't going to make that much of a difference," he told her, watching the rhythmic way her hips swayed as she made her way to the door. "In the long run, it won't get you there any faster."

Kansas didn't slow down. Entering the stairwell, she started down the stairs, her heels clicking on the metal steps.

"I know," she tossed over her shoulder. "I just need to be moving." She hadn't really meant to share that. What was it about this man that seemed to draw the words out of her? That seemed to draw out other things, too? "It makes me feel as if I'm getting something accomplished."

"We're going to catch him," Ethan told her with quiet affirmation once he reached the bottom step and was next to her.

She looked at him sharply, expecting to see that he was laughing at her and being condescending. But he wasn't. He looked sincere. Which either meant that he was or that he was a better actor than she'd initially given him credit for.

Kansas went on the offensive. "You don't really believe that."

"Actually," he told her, "I do." They went down another flight, moving even faster this time. "I just don't know how long it's going to take. The more fires there are, the more likely it is that he's going to trip up, show his hand, have someone catch him in the act. *Something*," he underscored, "is going to go wrong for him—and right for us."

Reaching the first floor, Kansas hurried to the front entrance. Not waiting for the others, she pushed it open with the flat of her hand.

"Meanwhile, the bastard's turning Aurora into a pile of ashes."

"Not yet," Ethan countered. They were outside, but she was still moving fast. Heading toward his car. He kept up with her. "I take it that you don't want to wait for the others."

"They'll meet us there," she said, reaching his vehicle.

His keys in his hand, he hit the remote button that disarmed the security device. Getting in, he shook his head. "Ever have a partner before?" he asked Kansas.

She got in and buckled up, tension racing through her body. She was anxious to get to the site of the fire, as if her presence there would somehow curtail any further harm the fire might render.

"I don't have one now," she pointed out glibly. As far as she was concerned, "temporary" didn't count.

The look Ethan gave her did something strange to her stomach. It felt as if she'd just endured an accelerated fifty-foot drop on a roller-coaster ride.

"Yeah," Ethan corrected, "you do. Better adjust," he advised mildly.

Mild or not, that got her back up. "And if I don't?" she challenged, unconsciously raising her chin as if silently daring him to take a swing.

"It'd just be easier on everyone all around if you did. We're all after the same thing," he reminded her not for the first time. "Nailing this creep's hide to the wall."

She began to retort, then thought better of it. The man was right. This was her frustration talking, not her. Taking a deep breath, she forced out the words that needed to be said. "You're right, I'm sorry."

He gave her a long glance. Had she just apologized to him? That wasn't like her. "Don't throw me a curve like that," he told her, and she couldn't tell if he was serious or not. "I'm liable to jump the divider and crash this beautiful car."

She noticed that he put the car first. The man really

was enamored with this cream-colored machine, wasn't he?

"Very funny," she cracked. "I admit I have a tendency to go off on my own, but it's just that I'm so damn frustrated right now," she told him. Then she elaborated: "We should have been able to find him by now. *I* should have been able to find him by now."

"No, you had it right the first time," he said quietly. "*We* should have been able to find this sicko by now."

She was out of ideas and her brain felt as dry as the Mojave Desert. "What are we doing wrong?"

"I don't know," he admitted.

There was a long moment of silence, and then he became aware of Kansas suddenly straightening in her seat. He was beginning to be able to read her. And she'd just thought of something. He'd bet money on it.

"Talk," he told her. "What just suddenly occurred to you?"

So excited by what she was thinking, she could hardly sit still. But she answered Ethan's question with one of her own. "Do we have any footage of the crowds that gathered around to see the outcome of these fires?"

"*We* don't, but I'm sure the local news stations do. This is the kind of story that they live for." With each fire, the coverage became that much more intense, lasting that much longer. He'd never known that so much could be said about any given topic. The media were in a class by themselves.

She didn't care about the press. Reporters who earned a living focusing on people in possibly the worst moments of their lives had always struck her as annoying at best. At worst they were vultures. But right now, they could unwittingly provide a useful service.

"Do you think we can get our hands on some of that footage?"

He personally couldn't, but he figured Dax could. Or, if not him, then certainly the chief of D's could. "Don't see why not." It didn't take much to figure out where she was going with this. "You think our firebug's in the crowd?"

She never liked committing herself, even though her answer was yes. "Worth a look."

Ethan nodded. "I'll ask Dax to requisition as much footage from each fire as is available. If he can't, the chief can. I'll tell him it's your idea," he added, just in case she thought he might be tempted to steal her thunder.

Because O'Brien was being magnanimous, she could return the favor, all the while reminding herself not to let her guard down. That would be a mistake.

"*Our* idea," she corrected. "We were brainstorming. Kind of."

Ethan grinned. "You just might make it as a team member yet, Kansas."

"Something to shoot for," she allowed. Although she damn well knew that by the time she'd adjusted to being "one of the guys," or whatever O'Brien wanted to call it, she'd be back at the firehouse, working on her own again.

It might, she couldn't help thinking as she stole a side glance at Ethan, actually take a little adjusting on her part to make the transition back.

Who would have ever thought it?

When they arrived at the site of the newest fire some fifteen minutes later, chaos had settled in. The rather small front lawn before the nursing home was completely littered with vintage citizens, many of whom, despite the hour, were in their pajamas and robes. A number were confined to wheelchairs.

She saw several of the latter apparently on their own, deposited haphazardly away from the fire. One resident looked absolutely terrified. There weren't nearly enough aides and orderlies, let alone nurses, to care for or reassure them.

As she started toward the terrified, wild-eyed old woman, Kansas's attention was drawn away to the almost skeletal-looking old man who was lying on the grass. There was a large and burly firefighter leaning over the unconscious resident, and she could tell from the fireman's frantic motions that the old man's life hung in the balance.

Kansas held her breath as the firefighter, his protective helmet and gloves on the ground, administered CPR. He was doing compressions on the frail chest and blowing into the all-but-lifeless mouth.

A distressed nurse was hovering beside the firefighter like an anemic cheerleader, hoarsely giving instructions as he worked over the senior citizen.

"Now that's really odd," Kansas muttered under her breath.

Before Ethan could ask her what she meant, Kansas was already working her way through the crowd and over to the scene. By the time she reached them, the firefighter had risen unsteadily to his feet. His wide face was drawn and he was clearly shaken.

"I lost him," he lamented in disbelief. The anguished words weren't addressed to anyone in particular, but more to the world in general. It was obvious that the towering firefighter was berating himself for not being able to save the old man. "I lost him," he cried again, his voice catching. "Oh God, I lost him."

With effort, the nurse dropped to her knees. Steadying herself, she pressed her fingers against the elderly man's throat, searching for any sign of a pulse. She didn't find it.

The nurse sighed, shaking her head. Her next words confirmed what had already been said. "Mr. Walters is gone." Looking up at the fireman, in her next breath she absolved him of any blame. "You did everything you possibly could."

"I didn't do enough," the firefighter protested. He looked defeated and almost lost.

"Yes, you did," the nurse said with feeling. She held her hand up to him and the distraught firefighter helped her to her feet. "Don't beat yourself up about it. It was Mr. Walters's time."

The next moment, a reporter with one of the local stations came running over to the firefighter and the nurse. His cameraman was directly behind him. Thrusting his microphone at the duo, the reporter began firing questions at them, ready and willing to turn this tragedy into a human-interest sound bite in a blatant attempt to be the lead story of the hour tonight.

Kansas noted that the firefighter looked even more anguished than he had a few moments earlier as he began to answer the reporter's questions.

She glanced over toward Ethan, who had caught up to

her again. "What do you make of that?" she murmured in as discreet a voice as she could manage and still be heard above the din.

Ethan wasn't sure where she was trying to go with this. "He's obviously someone who takes his job to heart." He saw the number on the engine and knew that she'd come from that fire station. "I take it that you don't know him."

Kansas shook her head. "He came to the house just when I got promoted to investigator. I hang out at the firehouse, but I have my own office, do my own thing. They answer the calls, I only go if arson's suspected." She pressed her lips together. "I'm really not part of that whole firefighting thing anymore."

Ethan detected something in her voice. "Do you miss it?"

He had a feeling he knew the answer to that no matter what she said. He was prepared for her to say something dismissive in response. He'd come to learn that she was nothing if not a private person. Ordinarily, that would be a signal for him to back off.

But she intrigued him.

"Sometimes," she murmured in a low voice, surprising him. "Other times, I feel I'm doing more good as an investigator. Or at least I was before this lunatic showed up, setting fire to everything in his path and driving me crazy. Us," Kansas amended quickly. "Driving us crazy."

Thinking in the plural was harder than she'd realized. It was really going to take practice.

Ethan grinned, appreciating the effort she was making. He couldn't help wondering if she was just turning over a new leaf or if she was doing this solely because of what he'd said earlier.

"You're coming along, Kansas. You're coming along."

She had no idea why his approval didn't incense her. Why it had, oddly enough, the exact opposite effect. Maybe she'd been breathing in too much smoke these last few years, she theorized.

About to say something flippant about his comment, Kansas stopped as she became aware that the rest of the task force had just joined her and Ethan.

The moment they had, Ethan went to Dax and she knew without having to listen in that he was making the request for the available footage of the last dozen fires. She couldn't help smiling to herself as she made her way over to the two men.

They looked alike, she caught herself thinking. Both dark, both good-looking. On a scale of 1 to 10, they were both 10s. With Ethan possibly being a 10.5.

And what did *that* have to do with the price of tea in China? she upbraided herself. She needed to stay focused and not let her mind wander like this.

When she was within earshot, she heard Dax ask her partner, "You think he stuck around to watch the fire department try to save the buildings?"

"The minute Kansas said it, it made sense. I'm sure of it," Ethan told Dax vehemently. "He wouldn't be able to resist. This is like an opiate to him. It's too much of a draw for him to pass up."

"Okay," Dax agreed. "I've got a few connections. I'll see what I can do."

"I've got a smartphone," Ethan suddenly remembered as Dax began to walk to his car.

Youngman looked at him oddly. "As opposed to what, a stupid phone?"

"No, you idiot," Ortiz, years younger than the veteran detective, berated his partner in disgust. "He means he's got a video camera in it."

Ethan was already putting his phone to use, panning the surrounding area and committing the image to film. It was a very simple act. He sincerely hoped it would help in capturing what was turning out to seem like a very complex perp.

"I believe this comes under the heading of 'be careful what you wish for,'" Dax announced the following morning as he walked up to Kansas's desk and deposited a huge carton. The carton was filled to the brim with videotapes.

She had to rise from her chair in order to see inside the box. "What's all this?" she asked.

"These are the tapes you asked for," he reminded her. "This is all footage from the fires."

"All these?" she asked incredulously, having trouble processing the information. There was an incredible amount of footage to review, she thought with a sinking feeling.

"No. That's only a third. Youngman and Ortiz are bringing the other two boxes."

She groaned as she took out the first tape. It looked as if her eyes were about to become tread-worn.

## Chapter 9

"What are you doing?" Kansas asked in surprise.

On her feet, she'd picked up the first box of tapes that Dax had gotten for her to review. Braced for hours of incredible boredom, she was about to head to the small, windowless room where a monitor, coupled with a VCR, was housed. Her question, and the surprise that had prompted it, was directed toward Ethan, who had just picked up one of the other boxes and was walking behind her.

"Following you," he said simply.

She immediately took that to mean that he thought she needed help transporting the tapes. It was inherently against her nature to allow anyone to think she wasn't capable of taking care of herself in any fashion.

Kansas lifted her chin. He was beginning to recognize that as one of her defensive moves. He really needed to find a way to get her to be more trusting, Ethan thought.

"I can carry them."

"I'm sure you can," he told her in an easygoing voice, but he couldn't help adding, "Probably with one hand tied behind your back." He gave her a weary look. "For once, why don't you just accept help in the spirit it's offered? This isn't any kind of a covert statement about your capabilities. I just thought I'd help you with them, that's all."

Kansas felt a flush of embarrassment. She supposed she was being a little paranoid. She was far more accustomed to put-downs than help. It hadn't been easy, even in this day and age, getting accepted in her chosen field. It was still, for all intents and purposes, mostly an all-boys club. Female firefighters and female arson investigators were a very small group, their authority and capabilities challenged almost at every turn.

"Sorry," she murmured in a small voice as she resumed walking. "Thank you."

Ethan nodded. "Better." Grinning, he fell into place beside her as they went down the hall. "I thought I'd give you a hand viewing them. There're two monitors in the room and two sets of eyes are better than one."

She hadn't realized that there were two monitors, but even if she had, she wouldn't have expected anyone else to volunteer for the tedious job of looking for the same face to pop up somewhere within every crowd shot of the various fires.

She stopped walking and looked at him in astonishment. "You're actually volunteering, of your own free will, to help me go over the tapes?"

Arriving at the room, he shifted the box to one side, balancing it on his hip in order to open the door for her. He stepped back and allowed her to go in first. "I think if you play back the conversation, that's what I just said."

Walking in, she deposited the box on the long, metal-top table that served as a desk. Both monitors with their VCRs were on it.

"Why?" she asked, turning to face him.

He put down his box next to hers. "Because that's what partners do, and like I said, for better or for worse, we're temporary partners." He pulled out his chair and sat down. "The sooner we get done with these, the sooner we can move on to something else. Maybe even catching this guy," he added.

Considering the way she'd treated him, O'Brien was being incredibly nice. She wondered if it were a mistake, letting her guard down just a little. She didn't like leaving herself open. But verbally sparring with him after his offer of help didn't seem right, either.

"Thank you," she finally said. "That's very nice of you."

He took out the first tape. The writing on the label was exceptionally neat—and small. An ant would need glasses to read it, he thought.

Ethan gave her a glance. "Remember that the next time you want to take my head off."

She supposed she had that coming. She hadn't exactly been the most easygoing, even-tempered person to work with.

"It's not your fault, you know," she murmured, sitting down. "The way I react."

"Never thought it was," he answered glibly. Ethan paused, waiting. But she didn't say anything further. So he did. "Okay, whose fault is it?"

Again, Kansas didn't answer right away. Instead, she seemed to be preoccupied with taking tapes out of the box and arranging them in some preordained order on the long, narrow table that they were using. It was a balancing act at best. Most of the space was taken up by the monitors. She remained silent for so long, Ethan decided she wasn't going to answer him.

And then she did.

"My husband's," she replied quietly. "It's my husband's fault."

Ethan stared at her. To say he was stunned would have been a vast understatement. His eyes instantly darted to Kansas's left hand. There was no ring there, which caused another host of questions to pop up in his head. Men didn't always wear a wedding ring. Women, however, usually did. But she didn't have one.

"You're married?" he asked, the words echoing in the small room.

"Was," Kansas corrected him. "I *was* married. A long time ago." She took a breath, because this wasn't easy to admit, even to herself, much less to someone else. But he was still a stranger, which in an odd way made it somewhat easier. "Biggest mistake of my life."

The statement instantly prompted another thought. "He abused you?"

The moment the words were out of his mouth, Ethan felt himself growing angry. Growing protective of her. The only other time he'd ever felt that way was when his mother had told them about their father. About being abandoned by the only man she'd ever loved, which to him represented abuse of the highest degree.

"Not physically," Kansas was quick to answer. Which only led him to another conclusion.

"Emotionally?"

She laughed shortly, but there was no humor in the sound. "If you call bedding the hotel receptionist on our honeymoon emotional abuse, then yes, Grant abused me emotionally." And broke her heart, but she wasn't about to say that part out loud. That was only for her to know, no one else.

She knew that kind of thing couldn't just happen out of the blue. A guy didn't become worthless scum after he pledged to love, honor and cherish. The seeds had to have been there to begin with.

"You didn't have a clue what he was like before that?"

Yes, she supposed, in hindsight, she had. But she was so desperate to have someone love her that she'd disregarded any nagging doubts she had, telling herself that it would be different once they were married.

Except that it wasn't. It just got worse. So she'd ended it. Quickly.

Kansas shrugged carelessly. "I was in love and I made excuses for him."

Ethan looked at her for a long moment. She didn't strike him as the type who would do that. Obviously he was wrong. His interest as well as his curiosity was piqued a little more.

"If he came back into your life right now," Ethan asked, selecting his words carefully as he continued unpacking tapes and lining them up in front of him, "and said he was sorry, would you take him back?"

Kansas regretted having said anything. He was asking a question that was way too personal, but she couldn't blame him. This was all her fault. She'd opened the door to this and O'Brien was doing what came naturally to him—prying. And besides, the man *was* being helpful to her. She supposed she owed him the courtesy of an answer.

"That depends," she said tentatively.

He raised a quizzical brow. Definitely not what he would have expected her to say. He decided to push it a little further. "On what?"

And that was when he saw the lightning flash in her eyes. "On whether or not I could find a big enough barbecue skewer to use so that I could roast him alive."

Now *that* he would have expected to hear, Ethan thought, doing his best to keep a straight face. "I had no idea you were so bloodthirsty."

"I'm not," she admitted after a beat, "but he wouldn't know that—and I'd want him to sweat bullets for at least a while."

Ethan didn't even try to hold the laughter back. "How long did you stay married?" he asked once he finally sobered a little.

Kansas didn't answer him immediately. She hadn't talked about her short stint as a married woman to anyone. In a way, it almost felt good to finally get all this out. "Just long enough to file for a divorce."

That, he thought, explained a lot. "Is that what has

you so dead set against the male species?" he asked, voicing his thoughts out loud.

"Not all of it," she corrected. "Only the drop-dead handsome section of the species." Her eyes narrowed as she looked at him. "Because drop-dead handsome guys think they can get away with anything."

She was looking at him as if she included him in that small, exclusive club. But there was no way to ask her without sounding as if he had a swelled head. Ethan opted for leaving it alone, but he couldn't resist pointing out the obvious. "You can't convict a section of the population because one guy acted like a supreme jerk and didn't know what he had."

"And what is it that you think he had?" The question came out before she could think to bank it down. Damn it, he was going to think she was fishing for a compliment. Or worse, fishing for his validation. Which she didn't need, she thought fiercely. The only person's validation she needed was her own.

"A woman of substance," Ethan told her, his voice low, his eyes on hers. "You don't just make a commitment to someone and then fool around."

*No, he's just trying to suck you in. He doesn't mean a word of it.*

"And you, if you make a commitment, you stick to it?" she asked, watching his eyes. She could always tell when a man was lying.

"I've never made a commitment," he told her honestly. "It wouldn't be fair to have a woman clutching to strings if there weren't any."

Why was her breath catching in her throat like that? This was just talk, nothing more. There was absolutely no reason for her to feel like this, as if her pulse were just about to be launched all the way to the space station.

Shifting, trying to regain her bearings, her elbow hit one of the tapes and sent it falling to the floor. She exhaled, and bent down to pick it up. So did Ethan. They very narrowly avoided bumping heads.

But other body parts were not nearly so lucky. Stooping, their bodies brushed against one another, sending electric shock waves zipping through both of them at the same time. Kansas sensed this because just as she sucked in her breath, she thought she heard him do the same, except more softly.

When their eyes locked, the circuit seemed absolutely complete. Rising up, his hands on either side of her shoulders as he brought her up to her feet, Ethan didn't think his next move through, which was highly unlike him. What he did was go with instincts that refused to be silenced.

Ethan bent his head, lightly brushing his lips against hers. And then he savored a second, stronger wave of electricity that went jolting through his system the moment he made contact.

He would have gone on to deepen the kiss, except that was exactly the moment that Dax chose to walk in with the third box of tapes.

Dax looked from his cousin to the fire department loan-out. It didn't take a Rhodes Scholar to pick up the vibes that were ricocheting through the small room. The vibes that had absolutely nothing to do with the apprehension of a firebug.

Clearing his throat, Dax asked a nebulous question.

"Either of you two need a break?" His tone was deliberately mild.

Ethan glanced at her, then shook his head. "No, we're good," he assured Dax.

*Yes, he certainly is,* Kansas couldn't help thinking. Even a mere fleeting press of his lips to hers had told her that.

She was definitely going to have to stay alert at all times with this one, she thought. If she wasn't careful, he was going to wear away all of her defenses in the blink of an eye without really trying.

This was not good.

And she didn't know if she believed him about not making any false promises. He sounded convincing, but it could all be for show, to leave her defenseless and open. After all, she didn't really know the man.

But she knew herself.

It wasn't in her to play fast and loose no matter how much she wanted to. She wasn't the kind who went from man to man, having a good time with no thought of commitment. If she succumbed to this man, it would be a forever thing, at least on her part. And she already knew that there was no such word as *forever* in O'Brien's vocabulary.

"Good." She seconded Ethan's response when Dax turned his gaze in her direction.

"I'd send you a third pair of eyes." He addressed his remark to both of them, then waved at the equipment they were going to be using. "But there are only two monitors to be had."

"That's okay, Dax," Ethan answered for both of them. "We'll manage somehow."

"I'll hold you to that," Dax promised. Then, with a nod toward Kansas, he left the room, closing the door behind him. The lighting in the windowless room went from soft to inky.

It felt to Kansas that she'd been holding her breath the entire time. She stared at the door as if she expected it to open at any moment.

"Do you think that he saw us?" she asked Ethan uneasily.

"If he had, he would have said as much." There was no question in his mind about that. "Dax doesn't play games. None of the Cavanaughs do. They're all straight shooters."

She laughed softly, shaking her head. "That puts the lot of them right up there with unicorns, mermaids—and you."

He grinned at her. "Always room for more."

*What did that even mean?* she wondered. Was O'Brien just bantering, trying to tease her? Or was there some kind of hidden meaning to his words? What if he was saying that he and she could—

*Stop it. Don't be an idiot. That's just wishful thinking on your part. How many Grants do you need in your life before you finally learn? We come into this world alone and we leave it alone. And most of us spend the time in between alone, as well.*

"I'll have to get back to you on that," she told Ethan.

"Fair enough," he commented. And then he looked back at the piles of tapes. "We'd better get to work before Dax assigns us a keeper."

She merely nodded and applied herself to the task at hand.

And tried very, very hard not to think about the firm, quick press of velvet lips against hers.

"So?" Dax asked when Ethan and Kansas finally returned to their desks two days later and sank down in their chairs. They had brought in the boxes of tapes with them and deposited them on the floor next to their desks.

Ethan groaned, passing a hand over his eyes for dramatic effect. "I may never look at another TV monitor again."

There was only one way to take that comment. Disappointment instantly permeated the room. "Then you found nothing?"

"Nothing," Ethan confirmed. "Except that a lot of people could stand to have complete makeovers," he quipped.

Dax looked over toward the fire investigator. "Kansas, have you got anything more informative than that for me?"

She really wished she did. After all, looking through the crowd footage had been her idea. "No, I'm afraid not. Neither one of us saw anyone who turned up at all the fires—or even half of them," she added with an impatient sigh. "Because a lot of the fires took place in close proximity, there were some overlaps, the same people turning up at more than one blaze, but they definitely didn't pop up at enough fires for us to look for them and ask questions."

Dax didn't look as if he agreed with her. "How many overlaps?" he pressed.

"One guy turned up four times," Ethan interjected. Dax looked at him, listening. "Another guy, five. But five was the limit," he added. "Nobody showed up more than that."

Ethan opened his bottom drawer, looking for the giant bottle of aspirin. Finding it, he took it out. Then, holding it up, he raised an inquiring eyebrow in Kansas's direction.

Kansas nodded, the motion relatively restrained because of the headache that was taking over. Shaking out two pills, Ethan leaned over and placed them on her desk, along with an unopened bottle of water that seemed to materialize in his hands. She didn't know until then that he usually kept several such bottles on hand in his desk.

"So here we are again, back to square one," Ortiz complained, looking exceedingly frustrated. "No viable suspects amid the known arsonists and pyromaniacs, no firebug hanging around in the crowd, bent on watching his handiwork, secretly laughing at us."

Youngman added in his two cents. "Only good thing is that, except for that old man the other day, there haven't been any casualties at these fires."

Dax pointed out the simple reason for that piece of luck. "That's because the fire department always turns up quickly each and every time. Don't know how long that lucky streak's going to continue."

"Yeah, lucky for the people involved," Youngman commented, picking up on the key word. "Otherwise they'd most likely be being referred to in the past tense right about now."

Kansas began to nod, then stopped as Youngman's words as well as Dax's words replayed in her head. When they did and the thought occurred to her, she all but bolted ramrod straight in her chair.

Ethan noted the shift in her posture immediately. She'd thought of something, something they hadn't covered before. It surprised him how quickly he'd become in tune to her body language.

He told himself he was just being a good detective. "What?" he pressed, looking at Kansas.

She in turn looked around at the other three men on the task force. "Doesn't that strike anyone else as strange?" she wanted to know.

"What, that the fire department turned up at a fire?" Ortiz asked, not following her. "It's what they do." His puzzled expression seemed to want to know why she was even asking this question. "You of all people—"

But Ortiz didn't get a chance to finish.

"No," she interrupted, "the fire department turning up early. Each and every time. Doesn't that seem a little odd to anyone? It's the same firehouse that answers the call each and every time, as well." And it was her firehouse, which made her pursuing this line of questioning even worse.

"There're only two firehouses in Aurora," Dax pointed out. "These fires are taking place in the southern section."

She was well aware of that fact. And aware that in many towns, there *were* no fire departments with firefighters who were paid by the city. Instead, what the townships had were dedicated volunteers who responded to the call whenever it went out, no matter where they were and what they were doing. Aurora was lucky to have not one but two firehouses charged with nothing more than looking out for their citizens.

But these early responses were definitely a lot more than just happy coincidences. Something was off here.

"I know that. But getting there in time to save everyone, the odds start to rise against you when the number of occurrences goes up. And yet, each and every time, the fire department is practically there just as the fire starts."

Dax looked at her sharply. "What are you getting at, Kansas?"

She took a deep breath before saying it. And then she forced the words out. "That maybe whoever is setting these fires is one of the firefighters."

## Chapter 10

Her statement had gotten all four detectives to sit up and stare at her. Frustration and exhaustion were temporarily ousted.

"Do you know what you're saying?" Dax asked her incredulously.

Kansas nodded grimly. "I know *exactly* what I'm saying. But what other avenues are open to us?" She didn't want to think this way, but it had been a process of elimination. "The way I see it, it *has* to be one of the firefighters."

What she was suggesting was something no one wanted to think about or seriously consider.

"This is your own house you're pointing a finger at," Dax reminded her, clearly trying to wrap his mind around what she was saying.

The anguish was evident in her voice as she answered

him. "Don't you think I know that? Don't you think that I wish there was some other answer?"

"What makes you think *this* is the answer?" Dax persisted.

Telling him it was a feeling in her gut would only have the detectives quickly dismissing the idea. As far as they were concerned, she was the "new kid." And the new kid wasn't allowed to have gut feelings for at least a couple of years. So she cited the clinical reference she'd read about the condition.

"It's the hero syndrome," she replied simply.

Scratching the eight or nine hairs that still populated the top of his head, Youngman looked at his partner, who offered no insight. Youngman then looked at her.

"And the hero syndrome is?" he wanted to know.

To her surprise, Ethan took over just as she was about to explain. "That's when someone arranges events in order to come running to the rescue and have people regard him—or her—as a hero," he told the others. "Or like a nurse might fiddle with a patient's medication, making them code so that she can rush in with defibrillator paddles to bring them back from the brink of death. People like that get off playing the hero. It makes them feel important, like they matter." Finished, Ethan looked at Kansas. "That's what you mean, right?"

He explained it better than she could, she thought. Had he come across this before? "Right."

Dax seemed to be turning his cousin's words over in his head before asking his next question. "And just which of these firefighters do you think is capable of

She wished it was none of them, but she simply couldn't shake the feeling that it had to be.

"I don't know," she told Dax honestly. She was aware that all four pairs of eyes were on her, with perhaps Ethan's being the kindest. "Look, I hope I'm wrong, but if I am, then we're back to that damn square one again."

That suggestion was obviously more to Ortiz's liking. "It could still be a pyromaniac who just hasn't made the grid yet," he pointed out.

Ethan shot down his theory. "That's why Kansas and I just spent all those hours going over the news footage, looking for a face that might keep cropping up in the crowd shots. There wasn't any. The most hits we got were five." He repeated the information he'd already delivered once.

"So maybe these actually *were* just accidental, random fires," Ortiz suggested hopefully. "That kind of thing *does* happen around here."

"Then how do you explain the accelerants I found?" Kansas asked quietly.

"I forgot about that." Ortiz's shoulder slumped and he seemed to slide down a little farther in his chair. "I can't."

"You know those firefighters better than any of us," Dax pointed out, turning toward her again. Crossing his arms before him, pausing for a long moment, he finally asked, "How do you suggest we get started?"

When in doubt, go the simple route. Someone had once said that to her, she couldn't remember who. But she did remember that she'd taken it to heart and it had helped her see things through.

"Same way we'd get started with any suspects we're trying to rule out," she told the prime detective on the case. "Call them in and interview each of them one at a time."

Ortiz shook his head. "They're not going to cooperate," he predicted.

"They might," Ethan theorized. The others looked at him curiously. "If we ask the right questions, we should be able to get some idea of what's going on."

"Right questions," Ortiz echoed. "Such as?"

She'd already started forming them in her head. "Such as if they remember seeing anyone suspicious in the vicinity when they arrived. Or if they saw anything suspicious at all—coming, going, while they were there. Anything." She took a breath. This was the million-dollar question. "And if they thought that any of the other firefighters behaved with undue valor."

"You're going to question their bravery?" Ortiz asked in astonishment.

"Exactly," she answered.

Youngman shook his head, evidently foreseeing problems. "That'll make their radar go up immediately."

"We've got five interview rooms." Dax volunteered a fact they all already knew—with the exception of the fire investigator. "We divide and conquer and keep this under wraps."

"For as long as it takes to interview the first five firemen," Ortiz pointed out glumly. "After that, all hell's going to break loose. They'll talk."

Broad shoulders rose and fell. "Still better than nothing," Dax commented.

"I don't like this," Youngman protested. "Those guys risk their lives, running into a burning building when any sane person would run in the opposite direction as fast as they could—and now we're pointing fingers at them? Accusing them of actually *starting* the fire?"

"Not at *them,* at *one* of them," Kansas insisted.

Youngman frowned, clearly not won over. "I can't believe you just said that. You know how united those guys are. You focus on one of them, the rest close ranks around him, forming an impenetrable wall that's next to impossible to crack."

She pressed her lips together and nodded. "Yes, I know."

The older detective shifted in his seat, making direct eye contact with her. "And when they find out this is your idea," he predicted, "they're not going to be very happy."

She knew that, too. But she refused to let that dictate how she did her job. "Nothing I haven't encountered before," she replied quietly, bracing herself for what was to come.

Ethan was perched against her desk, leaning a hip against the corner. He had been observing her for a few minutes and now finally commented: "You know, if you shrug your shoulders just the right way, that big chip you're carrying around could very possibly fall off."

If there was something she hated more than criticism, she couldn't remember what it was. "I don't *have* a big chip," she insisted.

Ethan lifted his right shoulder in a timeless, careless shrug. "Then it's got to be the biggest dandruff flake I've ever encountered," he assessed.

Swallowing an exasperated sigh, she ignored him and instead looked at Dax. "I don't *want* to be right about this."

He could see by the look on her face that she was telling the truth.

"I know you don't," Dax commiserated. "For the time being, why don't you and Ethan re-canvass the areas of the last few fires, knock on the same doors, see if any of the stories have been altered this time around."

She saw through the suggestion. "I appreciate what you're trying to do, Detective Cavanaugh, but I really don't need to be shielded. I don't break. It's my suggestion, so I can handle my end of it."

Dax couldn't hide his concern. "I'm thinking about when this is all over and you have to go back."

So was she...for about a second. Why borrow trouble? It would be there waiting for her once this was over.

"I appreciate that, Detective, but I really can handle myself. Captain Lawrence is a fair man, and I don't really interact with the men on any sort of a regular basis anymore anyway." Kansas didn't realize at first that she was smiling as she looked around the squad room. "Not like I do here."

Dax allowed himself a small smile as he nodded. "All right, then. Since this involves possibly getting on the fire department's bad side, let me just run this by the chief of D's and see what he has to say about it." He looked around at the task force. "When he gives his okay, who wants to inform Captain Lawrence?"

She began to say that she would, but she wasn't fast enough. Ethan raised his hand and beat her to it. "I will."

"Hope you're up on your self-defense classes," Ortiz murmured.

Kansas swung around to look at her partner. "It's my idea. I'll do it." He began to say something, but she held up her hand to silence him. "They won't hit me. You, they just might."

Dax laughed. "She's got a point," he said to his cousin.

Ethan wasn't going to argue with him—and he knew better than to argue outright with her.

"Fine," Ethan compromised. "We'll both go."

He was adamant on that point. There was no way he was going to let her walk into the firehouse with this new twist like some lamb to the slaughter. Whether she liked it or not, he was her partner for the time being, and that meant he intended to have her back at all times.

Kansas waited until Dax left to talk to his father. "I don't need a keeper," she informed Ethan indignantly, keeping her voice low.

"Yeah, you do, but that's an argument for another day," he retorted. "Besides, we send you alone, we look like a bunch of chickens hiding behind a woman." He shook his head. "Ain't gonna happen."

She inclined her head. Much as she wanted to argue with him, she could see his point. "I didn't think of it that way."

And neither had he—until just now.

But Ethan merely nodded in response and kept his satisfied grin to himself.

Brian looked at his son thoughtfully. Dax had laid out the theory that Kansas had come up with and that

Ethan had backed as succinctly as possible. Finished, his son waited for a comment.

Instead, Brian gestured for him to take a seat. Once Dax did, he asked for his opinion. "So what do you think of this idea?"

Dax knew that this was a giant step they were taking, one that didn't allow for any backtracking. And if they were wrong, there was going to be hell to pay. There might be hell to pay even if they were right. No one took being a suspect well, and this would cause at least a temporary rift between the police and the fire departments.

All that considered, Dax said, "I think they might be onto something. We've followed up all the so-called tips that have been coming in from the public hotlines, and all we've done is go around in circles." He sighed. "And meanwhile, buildings keep being burned. After each fire, we haul out all the usual suspects, all the firebugs out on parole and the known pyromaniac wannabes and come up with nothing. They all make sure that they've always got an alibi."

"And the media footage?" Brian asked. It had taken a bit of persuading on his part to secure that from the various local stations. "Did that show up anything?"

Dax shook his head. "Different faces at different fires. If this firebug's doing it to get a rush, he's got some remote hook-up going to view the sites, because he's not showing up in the crowds."

They had no choice but to pursue this new avenue, Brian thought. They were out of options. "I'll talk to Captain Lawrence. Go ahead and question the firefighters. Just try to do it as delicately as possible," he cautioned, though he was fairly confident he didn't really have to. Dax had a good head on his shoulders. All the younger Cavanaughs did. "I don't want some yahoo getting it into his head to turn this into a feud between the Aurora Police Department and the fire department."

Dax was already on his feet and crossing to the door. "Don't worry, we'll do our best to be discreet," he promised.

"Oh, and, Dax?" Brian called out just as his son was about to walk out.

Stopping, Dax looked at his father over his shoulder. "Yes?"

"How's Ethan coming along?" This was the first time that Dax was working with the other detective, and Brian was curious about the way things were going between them. As a family, the three O'Briens and the Cavanaughs were all still getting accustomed to one another.

And that didn't even begin to take in the curveball that Andrew had thrown him the other week. That, Brian knew, was still under wraps as far as the rest of the family was concerned.

Dax grinned. "Just like you'd expect, Chief. Like a born Cavanaugh."

Brian nodded his head. "Good to hear." He had equally good reports on Kyle and Greer. At this point, it seemed as if the only one of them who had ever disappointed the family had been Mike, who'd ultimately never managed to conquer the demons he lived with. "Keep me apprised of the way the questioning is going," he requested. "And give me a holler if you need me," he added, raising his voice just before his son went down the hall.

Dax raised his hand over his head as he kept going. "Absolutely."

Brian crossed to the door and closed it. He knew that Dax wouldn't be coming to him with any problems. He'd raised them all to know that family was always there for them if the need arose but that they were expected to stand independently on their own two feet if at all possible. None of his sons, nor his daughter, had ever disappointed him.

And neither, he thought now, had Lila's four kids, whom he'd regarded as his own even before he and Lila had exchanged vows.

All in all, he mused, getting back to the report he'd been reading just before Dax came in, he was one hell of a lucky man.

Arms crossed before his barrel chest, covering the small drop of ketchup that recalled lunch and the fries he'd had, Captain John Lawrence was one frown line short of a glare as he regarded the young woman who'd spent the last four years assigned to his firehouse.

"What do you want to talk to them for?" he asked suspiciously, grinding out the words.

The smile on his lips as he'd greeted her and the detective she'd walked in with had quickly dissolved when she'd made her request to interview each of his men. Eyes the color of black olives shifted from Kansas to the man standing beside her and then back again, waiting.

Kansas tried again. She'd been the object of Lawrence's displeasure before, when she'd first been assigned to him. In time, she'd won him over. It looked now as if all her hard work and dedication had just been unraveled in the last couple of minutes.

"We're hitting a dead end," she explained patiently, "and we're hoping that one of them might have seen something that we didn't."

"They were kind of busy at the time," he pointed out. Lawrence didn't bother trying to mask the sarcasm in his voice.

"We appreciate that, Captain Lawrence," Ethan said respectfully but firmly. "But you never know what might help break a case. Sometimes the smallest, most inconsequential thing—"

Impatient, Lawrence waved a hand at him, dismissing the explanation. "Yeah, yeah, I know the drill—and the drivel," he added pointedly. He looked far from pleased. Just as it seemed that he was going to be stubbornly uncooperative, the captain grudgingly said, "If you really think it can help the investigation, I'll send them over to talk to you." He looked at Kansas and his expression softened, but only slightly. Ethan could see that she had fallen out of favor. With any luck, it was only temporary. "You want everybody?"

She gave him a little leeway. "Everybody who was on call for the fires."

The disgruntled expression intensified. "That's everybody."

"Wasn't it just one shift?" Ethan asked innocently. Most of the fires had taken place under the cover of twilight or later.

"They overlapped," the captain answered coldly. His

attention was back to Kansas. "Okay with you if I send just three at a time—barring a fire, of course," he added cynically.

Ethan ran interference for her, determined to take the brunt of the captain's displeasure. "Of course," he said. "Goes without saying. The fires always take precedent."

There was something akin to contempt in the captain's dark eyes as they swept over him. "Glad you agree," Lawrence finally commented. And then he asked Kansas, "Tomorrow okay with you? Most of the guys you want to talk to are off right now. It's been a rough few days."

In Ethan's opinion, it had been a rough few months. And besides, it was getting late anyway. He and Kansas were both off the clock and had been for the last half hour. Lawrence had kept them waiting almost an hour before he "found" the time to see them.

"Tomorrow's fine," Ethan answered. Leaning forward, he shook Lawrence's hand. "Thanks for your cooperation." He managed to say the words with a straight face.

"Hey, we're all on the same team, right?" It was hard to tell whether Lawrence was being serious or sarcastic, but Ethan was leaning toward the latter.

"Right," Kansas agreed.

It had earned her a less than warm look from the captain. She was in the doghouse and she knew it. It was obvious that the man was annoyed with her because she hadn't been able to somehow spare him what she was sure Lawrence saw as a major inconvenience.

She was equally sure that he didn't realize that his

men were under suspicion at the moment. Because if he had known, he would have said as much. Most likely at the top of his lungs while liberally sprinkling more than a few choice words throughout his statement. Lawrence wasn't the kind to keep things bottled up and to himself. If he was angry, *everyone* knew he was angry. They also knew about what and at whom. The man didn't believe in sparing feelings.

Taking their leave, Kansas and Ethan walked out of the fire station. Once outside, she turned to him and said, "You should have let me do the talking."

He'd done the brunt of it for a very simple reason. "You've got to come back here. I don't. I wanted Lawrence to think of me as the messenger in all this. When he realizes what's going on, he's not going to be a happy camper," Ethan predicted. "I don't want him taking it out on you."

Kansas looked at him, curbing her natural impulse to shrug off any offers of help and declare that she could take care of herself. If pressed, she would have to admit, if only to herself, that it was rather nice to have someone looking out for her. It was something she'd really never experienced before.

Her lips curved in a half smile as she said, "I guess chivalry isn't dead."

Smiling in response, Ethan lead the way across the parking lot to his car.

The fact that she'd accepted his help had him deciding to venture out a little further. He watched as she got in, then got in himself. His key in the ignition, he left it dormant for a moment and turned toward her.

"Feel like getting some dinner?" he asked her, then added, "We're off the clock."

A couple of weeks ago, she would have turned him down without a moment's hesitation. A couple of weeks ago, she *had* turned him down, she recalled.

But that was then, and this was now. And she really didn't feel like going home and being by herself. Not after the captain had just looked at her as if she were a leper.

"Sure, why not?"

He'd learned not to declare victory with her until he was completely certain of it. "You realize I don't mean a drive-through, right?"

Her smile widened. "I realize."

He found he had to force himself to look away. Her mouth could look very enticing when it wasn't moving. "Good. We're on the same page."

*Not yet,* she thought, a warmth slipping over her. But she had a feeling that they were getting there.

# Chapter 11

"You look like you could use a friend," Ethan commented as he sank down into his chair across from Kansas.

It was the end of yet another grueling day of interviews. For the last two days, he and Kansas had been questioning the firefighters who had been the first responders to each and every fire under investigation. The firefighters who, for the most part, she had once worked with side by side.

The interviews, as she'd expected, had not been a walk in the park. At best, the men were resentful and growing steadily more begrudging in their answers. At worst, the responses bordered on being insulting, hostile and verbally abusive. And Kansas, because she was considered one of them—or had been until now—had caught the worst of it.

It took her a moment now to realize that O'Brien was

talking to her. And then another moment to replay in her head what he'd just said.

"I could use a drink," she countered, closing her eyes and leaning back in her chair. Every muscle in her shoulders felt welded to the one next to it, forming knots the size of boulders. "And a friend," she added after a beat.

If he was surprised by the latter admission, he didn't show it. "I might have a solution for both," Ethan proposed. The comment had her opening her eyes again. "We're off duty." Technically, they'd been off for the last twenty minutes. "What do you say to stopping by Malone's?"

"I still have these reports to finish," she protested, indicating the daunting pile of files sitting in front of her on the desk.

Getting up, Ethan leaned over their joint desks and shoved the files over to the far corner.

"We're off duty," he repeated. Then, to make his point, he rounded their desks, got behind her chair and pulled it back so that she was actually sitting in the aisle rather than at her desk.

She looked over her shoulder at him. "What's Malone's?" she wanted to know.

Ethan took her hand, urging her to her feet. She had no choice but to acquiesce. "A haven," Ethan answered simply.

"A haven that serves drinks," Kansas amended in amusement.

"That's what makes it a *good* haven," he explained, a whimsical smile playing along his lips.

He'd become acquainted with Malone's the day he

became a detective. One of the other detectives invited him along for a celebratory drink in honor of his newly bestowed position. Malone's was a local gathering place, more tavern than bar. Detectives of the Aurora police force as well as various members of their family gravitated there for no other reason than to just be among friends who understood what it meant to be a police detective or part of a detective's family.

On any given evening, a healthy representation of the Cavanaughs could be found within the ninety-year-old establishment's four walls. He, Kyle and Greer had discovered that shortly after they'd discovered their new identities. Coming to Malone's helped bolster a sense of camaraderie as well as a sense of belonging.

"Are you up for it?" he prodded.

"If I say no, you won't give me any peace until I surrender." It wasn't a question, it was an assumption. O'Brien had definite pit bull tendencies. She could relate to that. "So I guess I might as well save us both some grief and say yes."

Ethan grinned, looking exceeding boyish. He didn't come across like someone to be reckoned with—but she knew he was.

"Good conclusion," he told her. He watched her close down her computer. "I can take you," he volunteered. "And then later I can bring you back to your car."

The last interview had gone exceptionally badly. Tom Williams, a man she had once regarded as a friend, had all but called her a traitor. She was feeling very vulnerable right now, and the last thing she wanted was to be in a car with Ethan when she felt like that. Major mistakes were built on missteps taken in vulnerable moments. If she hadn't felt so alone, she wouldn't have fallen for Grant like that.

"Why don't I just follow you and save you the trouble of doubling back," she countered.

"No trouble," he assured her, spreading his hands wide. The look on her face didn't change. "Have it your way," he declared, raising his hands up in mock surrender. "I'll lead the way." She had her purse, and her computer was powered down. He looked at her expectantly. "You ready?"

Kansas caught her bottom lip between her teeth. She supposed that one drink couldn't hurt. But one, she promised herself, was going to be her limit.

"Ready," she echoed.

It was a good plan, and had she stuck to it she would have been home at around the time she'd initially planned. In addition, there would have been plenty of time to get a good night's sleep. But she strayed from the path within the first fifteen minutes of arrival.

Because she'd felt as stiff as a rapier and really wanted to loosen up a little and fit in, she'd downed the first drink placed in front of her instead of sipping it. Ethan's cautionary words to go slow—something that surprised her—were ringing in her ears as she ordered a second drink. Maybe she'd ordered it *because* he'd warned her to go slow and she was feeling combative.

After facing what amounted to blatant hostility all day, being here, amid the laughter of friendly people in a warm atmosphere, was the difference between night and day. Reveling in it, she consequently let her guard down as she absorbed the warm vibrations of the people around her.

An hour into it, as more and more people filled the tavern, she turned to Ethan and whispered, "I can't feel my knees."

He hadn't left her side the entire time and had warned her against the last two of the three drinks she'd had. He looked down now, as if to verify what he was about to say. "They're still there," he assured her.

"I'm serious," she hissed. She didn't like this vague, winking-in-and-out feeling that had come over her. "What does that mean?"

This time he looked at her incredulously. She was serious. Who would have thought? "You've never been drunk before?"

"I'm drunk?" Kansas echoed, stunned. "You sure?" she questioned.

Suppressing his grin, Ethan held up his hand, folding down two fingers. "How many fingers am I holding up right now?"

Kansas squinted, trying her best to focus. Her best was not quite good enough. "How many chances do I get?"

He had his answer. "Okay, Cinderella, time for you to go."

Kansas tried to take a deep breath and began to cough instead. She was feeling very wobbly. "I don't think I can drive."

"No one was going to let you," he assured her. His tone was friendly but firm. He would have wrestled the keys away from her if he'd had to. "C'mon, let's go outside for some fresh air," he urged, slowly guiding her through the crowd.

She found that she had to concentrate very hard to put one foot in front of the other without allowing her knees to buckle. "I'd rather go somewhere more private. With you." Those were the words in her head. How they'd managed to reach her tongue and emerge, she really wasn't sure.

He nodded toward the room behind them teeming with people. "Right now, outside *is* more private. And I'll be coming with you. I'll be the one holding you up," he told her.

"Good," she said, "because I'm not altogether sure I can manage to do that on my own," she confessed. The second the words registered with her brain, she asked, "What did you put in my drink?"

"I didn't put anything into your drink," he told her, shouldering a path for her as he kept his arm around her waist. He caught Kyle looking his way—and smiling. "Could be that having three of them in a row might have had something to do with your knees dissolving on you."

Having made it to the front door, he pushed it open and guided her over the threshold. Once outside, he moved over to the side and leaned her against the wall in an effort to keep her upright and steady. He had the feeling that if he stepped back, she'd slide right down to the ground.

He was close to her. So close that his proximity worked its way into her system, undermining every single resolution she'd ever made.

God, he was handsome, she thought. Jarringly handsome.

"You know, you're just too damn good-looking for my own good."

*She would have never said that sober,* he thought. Ethan couldn't help the grin that came to his lips. "I'll remember you said that. You probably won't want me to, but I will." He put his arm up to hold her in place as she began to sink a little. "Take a deep breath," he instructed. "It'll help."

She did as he told her, which was when Ethan realized that his supporting arm was way too close to her chest. As she inhaled, her breasts rose, making contact with his forearm.

All sorts of responses went ricocheting through Ethan.

"Maybe not quite so deep," he suggested.

She was very aware of the contact. And equally aware of what it was doing to her.

"Why?" she asked, cocking her head as she looked at him, her blond hair spilling out onto his arm like soft fairy dust. "Am I getting to you, Detective O'Brien?"

*She has no idea, does she?* he thought. "You need to sleep this off," he informed her.

Her eyes were bright as she asked, "You're taking me home?"

"Yes." And then, to make sure that there wasn't any confusion about this, he added, "Your home."

Kansas sucked in another deep, deep breath. "'K," she agreed glibly.

Weaving one arm around her waist again, Ethan began to usher her to his car. While trying to maneuver,

Kansas got the heel of her shoe caught in a crack in the asphalt. She kept moving, but the shoe didn't, and she wound up dipping forward. Sensing she was about to fall, Ethan tightened his hold around her waist, dragging her closer against him.

For one second, their faces were less than a measurable inch away from one another.

And the next second, even that was gone.

Giving in to the moment and her weakened state of resistance, Kansas kissed him. Not lightly as she had in the kiss they'd previously shared, but with all the feeling that Ethan had stirred up within her. The alcohol she'd consumed had eroded her defenses and melted the distance she'd been determined to keep between herself and any viable candidate for her affections. Kansas wrapped her arms around his neck as she leaned into his very hard body. Leaned into the kiss that was swallowing them both up.

For a single isolated moment in time, Ethan let himself enjoy what was happening. Enjoy it and savor it because almost from the beginning, he'd wondered what it would be like to *really* kiss this vibrant woman who had for reasons that were far beyond him been thrust into his world.

Now he had his answer.

The kiss packed a wallop that left him breathless... and wanting more. Definitely more.

Which was when the warning flares went up.

This wasn't just something to enjoy and move on. This was something that created intense cravings that would inevitably demand to be filled.

As heat engulfed his body, he knew he had to tear

himself free—or else there very likely would be no turning back. And if he was going to make love with this woman, it was *not* going to be because her ability to reason had been diluted by something that came out of a bottle marked 90 proof.

Expending more self-control and effort than he ever had before, Ethan forcibly removed her arms from around his neck, broke contact and took a less than steady step back.

Bewilderment crossed her face. How could she have been so wrong? It was only because she was still inebriated that she had the nerve to ask, "You don't want me?"

He heard the confusion and hurt in her voice. "Not on my conscience, no."

His keys already in his hand, he pointed them toward his car, pressed the button and released the locks a second before he gingerly turned her toward his vehicle. Ethan opened the door and then very carefully lowered her onto the passenger seat. When she merely sat there, he ushered in her legs, shifting her so that she faced forward.

Hurrying around the back of the car, Ethan got in on the driver's side.

"You don't want me," she repeated in a soft, incredulous voice that was barely above a whisper. "God, I'm such an idiot," she upbraided herself.

Sticking the key in the ignition, he left it there and turned toward her. Maybe it was safer to have her think that, but the hurt in her voice was more than he could live with.

"Look, on a scale of one to ten, wanting you comes

in at fifteen," he told her. "But I want you because *you* made the decision to be with me. I don't want you making love with me because the decision was made for you by your alcohol consumption."

She stopped listening after the first part. "Fifteen?" she questioned as he started the engine.

"Yeah," he bit off, frustration eating away at him. There were times he wished he wasn't such a damn Boy Scout—even if his reasoning was dead on. "Fifteen."

Kansas took a deep breath, smiling from ear to ear with deep satisfaction. Sliding down in her seat, she stretched like a cat waking from a long, invigorating nap in the sun.

She had the grace of a feline as well, Ethan thought, trying—and failing—to ignore her.

She slanted a coy glance at him. "I can live with that."

He only wished he could.

But he was going to have to, he lectured himself. He had no other choice.

The most intense part of her buzz had worn off by the time Ethan made the turn that brought them into her garden apartment complex.

Her knees, she noted, were back, as were some of her inhibitions. But there was something new in the mix as well: surprise steeped in respect.

Ethan could have easily taken advantage of her temporary mindless condition. She'd all but thrown herself at him. Had he been anyone else, he could have very easily taken her to the backseat of his car and had sex with her, then crowed about it later to his friends.

That he didn't left her feeling grateful—and feeling something more than just simple attraction.

There was nothing simple about what was going on inside her.

The emotion was vaguely familiar, yet at the same time it was as new as the next sunrise. And she had no idea what to make of it, what to do about it or where to go from here. It was all just one great big question mark for her.

That, and an itch that all but begged to be scratched.

"Where can I park the car?" he asked her as they drove past a trove of daisies, their heads bowed for the night.

"Guest parking is over there." She pointed to a row of spaces, some filled, some not, that ran parallel to the rental office just up ahead.

Ethan took the first empty spot he came to. After pulling up the hand brake, he put the car into Park and turned off the engine. Getting out, he rounded the rear of the vehicle and came around to her side. He opened the door and took her hand to help her out.

She placed her hand in his automatically. The semi-fog around her brain was lifting, enabling her to focus better, physically and mentally. When she did, she had to squelch her initial impulse to just get out on her own and she took his hand, allowing him to help her. She knew she needed it.

There was something comforting about the contact, about having someone there with her, that she couldn't deny. That she *had* been denying herself, she thought, ever since she'd run from her disastrous, abbreviated marriage.

She raised her eyes to his as she got out. "Thanks," she murmured.

His smile was slow, sensual and instantly got under her skin. "Don't mention it."

Instead of getting into the car again as she'd expected, Ethan remained at her side. Nodding toward the array of apartments, he asked, "Which one is yours?"

"Number eighty-three," she told him, pointing toward the second grouping of apartments.

As he began walking in that direction, Ethan took her arm and held on to it lightly. He was probably worried that she was going to sink again, she thought. Kansas took no offense. How could she? Her limbs had been the consistency of wet cotton less than half an hour before. He was being thoughtful.

And getting to her more than she cared to admit.

Reaching her door, he waited until she took out her key and unlocked it.

"You going to be all right?" he asked.

The words "of course" hovered on her lips, straining to be released. It was the right thing to say. What she would have normally said.

But instead, what came out was, "Maybe you should walk me in, just in case."

Her eyes met his and there was a long moment that stretched out between them. A moment with things being said without words.

And then he inclined his head.

"All right."

# *Chapter 12*

The second Kansas stepped across her threshold into her apartment, she felt her adrenaline instantly kicking in. It raced madly to all parts of her at once, sounding a multitude of alarms like so many tiny Paul Reveres riding in the night. Her whole body went on alert—not in waves, but simultaneously.

The feeling intensified when she heard the lock click into place as Ethan closed the door behind him.

*This is it,* she thought. *Time to fish or cut bait, Beckett.*

She wanted to fish. Desperately.

*Damn it,* Ethan thought as a warmth undulated through his body, why was he doing this to himself? Why was he testing himself this way? He should have just ushered Kansas in, politely said good-night and then gotten out of there.

For every moment he hesitated, every moment that

he *didn't* do the right thing, it became that much harder for him to walk away.

But as much as he wanted her—and until this very moment he had no idea that he could possibly *ever* want a woman this much—he couldn't allow himself to act on that desire. He had a sister. If someone had taken advantage of her in this kind of a situation, he would have cut the guy's heart out and served it to him for lunch. Just because he was on the other side of this scenario didn't make it any more excusable for him to take advantage of the woman.

"So, if you're okay, I'll be going," he said, fully expecting his feet to engage and begin moving back to the door.

But they didn't move. They seemed to remain glued in place.

Kansas looked up at him. How could she be getting more beautiful, more desirable by the second? It wasn't possible.

And yet...

"But I'm not okay," she said.

The drinks she'd had at Malone's were probably getting to her stomach, Ethan guessed. "What's wrong? You feel sick?" He should have never brought her there, he upbraided himself.

"That wouldn't be the word I'd use," she answered, moving closer to him, dissolving the tiny distance between them until there wasn't space enough for a heartbeat.

As she began to put her arms around his neck, Ethan stopped her, catching her wrists and bringing her arms down again. He saw confused frustration crease Kansas's brow.

"In case you haven't noticed, Detective," she told him, "I'm throwing myself at you."

"Oh, I've noticed, all right." He'd been acutely aware of everything about her from the first moment. "And at any other time, I'd be more than happy to do the catching."

Her eyes narrowed as she struggled to understand. She took his words at face value. "What's wrong with Thursdays?"

He laughed softly, shaking his head. "There's nothing wrong with Thursdays. There's something wrong with taking advantage of a woman." He appealed to her because he really needed help if he was going to do the right thing. He couldn't do it on his own. He was only human. "Kansas, you're not thinking clearly. You're probably not thinking at all," he amended.

Otherwise, he reasoned, she wouldn't be acting this way. The Kansas he'd come to know wouldn't have thrown herself at a man. She would have skewered him if he even attempted anything.

Kansas took a breath, absorbing this. Men like O'Brien weren't supposed to exist. Everything she'd ever learned pointed to the fact that they didn't. And yet, here he was, sounding as noble as if he'd just ridden in on a charger with Lancelot.

No, with Galahad, she silently corrected herself, because Lancelot lusted after the queen, but Galahad was purity personified.

Looking Ethan squarely in the eye, she said, "Give me a calculus problem."

Just how hard had those three drinks hit her?
"What?"

"A calculus problem," she repeated. "If I solve it, will
that prove to you that my brain is functioning? That it
isn't in a fog and neither am I? I admit the drinks hit me
hard at first," she said before he could bring it up, "but
the effect didn't last, and believe me, that 'I can touch
the sky' feeling is long gone." Although, she thought,
it had served its purpose. "While it lasted, it let me say
what I couldn't say stone-cold sober. That I want to
make love with you."

Pausing for a moment, she looked up at him. Every
breath she took registered against his body, against his
skin.

"Don't you want to make love with me?" she asked
as the silence stretched out between them.

Oh God, did he ever. "You have no idea," he told her,
feeling as if the effort to restrain himself was all but
strangling him.

The smile that slipped over her lips in almost slow
motion drew him in an inch at a time. Trapping him so
that he couldn't turn back, couldn't cut loose. Couldn't
tear his eyes away.

She rose up on her toes. "Then educate me," she
whispered, her lips all but brushing against his as she
spoke.

He was just barely holding on to his self-control. The
next second, as the promise of her mouth whispered
along his, his self-control snapped in two, leaving him
without any resources to use in the fight against his
reactions.

Instead of doing the noble thing and protesting, or

saying anything about the way she was going to regret this, Ethan pressed his lips against hers and kissed her. *Really* kissed her.

Kissed her so deeply and with such feeling that he was instantly lost.

All he could think of was having her. Having her in the most complete, satisfying sense of the word and steeping himself in her until he wouldn't be able to tell where he ended and she began.

The kiss went deeper.

*Yes!*

The single, triumphant word echoed over and over again in Kansas's brain even as she felt her body melting in the flames that his mouth had created within her. This, this was the connection she'd missed, the part of herself she had struggled to pretend didn't exist, the part of her that hadn't been allowed to see the light of day. It broke free and filled every single space within her.

Everything within Kansas hummed with a happiness she hadn't known was achievable.

But as that feeling of happiness, of absolute joy, progressed, all but consuming her, Kansas swiftly came to realize that this really *wasn't* the feeling she'd hoped for.

This was more.

So very much more.

Before this, any kind of happiness she'd experienced with Grant amounted to little more than a thimbleful in comparison. This "thing" she was feeling was like an ocean. An all-encompassing, huge ocean. And she was swimming madly through it as the current kept sweeping her away, taking absolutely all control out of her hands.

She was at its mercy.

And she loved it!

She felt Ethan's breath on her neck, making her skin sizzle.

Making her want more.

And all the while the very core of her kept quickening in anticipation of what was to be. What she *hoped* was to be.

She struggled to hold herself at bay, struggled to savor this for as long as she could. For as long as it went on. Because something told her that these conditions would never be met again. This was a one-of-a-kind, one-time-only thing. Like the sighting of a comet.

And then, just like that, Ethan was no longer kissing her. His lips were no longer grazing the side of her neck, rendering her all but mindless. Ethan had drawn back, cupping her face in his hands as he silently declared a "time-out."

Confused, with shafts of disappointment weaving through her, she looked at Ethan quizzically. "What?" she asked breathlessly. Had she done something wrong? Turned him off somehow?

"Last chance," he offered.

She shook her head, not understanding. "Last chance for what?"

"For you to back out." He held his breath, waiting for her answer. Praying she'd say what he wanted her to say.

It came in the form of a soft laugh. The sound all but

ricocheted around her small living room. "Not on your life."

He couldn't begin to describe the urge he felt just then.

"Okay, just remember, I gave you a chance. You asked for this," he told her, his voice gruff.

"I know," she managed to say before her lips became otherwise engaged.

The next moment, his mouth was back on hers, kissing her senseless as his fingers got busy removing the layers of her clothing that were between them.

He began with her jacket, sliding it down her arms. The garment was followed by her cherry-red tank top and her white skirt. With each piece of clothing he removed from her, the heat encircling her intensified. And his breathing grew shorter, she noted, as a haze began to descend over her brain.

Refusing to be passive, even if she was being reduced to a mass of fiery yearning, Kansas started to remove his clothes, as well. As she worked buttons free, took down zippers, she felt as if her fingers were clumsier at this process than his were. But then, it wasn't as if she was altogether clear-headed right now. Or experienced at doing this kind of thing.

They achieved their goal at the same time.

Clothes commingling in a pile on the floor, their bodies primed and aching, he swept her into his arms as if she weighed no more than one of the reports that she'd left abandoned on the desk at the precinct.

"Where's your bedroom?" he asked in between pleasuring her mouth with bone-melting kisses.

"At the end of the hall," she answered with effort.

Because her lips had been separated from his during this short verbal exchange, Kansas framed his face with her hands, held his head in place as she raised up her mouth to cover his.

He almost dropped her. But that was because she was so effectively weakening his limbs.

Bringing her into her bedroom, he placed her on the bed, joining her without breaking rhythm. Ethan began kissing her with even more passion.

He made her forget absolutely everything, especially the glaring looks and thinly veiled derogatory remarks she'd received from this afternoon's collection of firefighters.

Nothing else mattered. Not her past, not the lonely isolation of her childhood, nor the emptiness of her short-lived marriage to a narcissist. All that mattered was sustaining this incredible feeling that was crescendoing through her.

Because of him.

In response to him, her own kisses became more passionate, more intense. Each place that Ethan touched, she mirrored the gesture, sweeping soft, questing fingertips over his tantalizingly hard body. Glorying in the way he responded to her, the way he moved. The sound of his moan drove her crazy.

She saw that she could arouse him even more with just a touch—just the way he could her. The thought of exercising that kind of control over him was mind-blowing. She felt like an equal, not just like a receptive vessel. That was the moment that this completely transcended anything she'd ever experienced before.

Thinking that she was at the highest level she could

reach short of the final one, she discovered in the next moment that she was wrong.

She all but lost the ability to snatch a thought out of the air when Ethan began to trace a hot, moist path to her very core, first with his hands and then, very swiftly, with his lips.

Suppressing a surprised gasp, Kansas was barely able to breathe as she rode the crest of the all-consuming climax Ethan had just produced within her.

She arched and bucked, desperate to absorb the sensation and keep it alive for even so much as a heartbeat longer. But when it left, leaving her convinced that she'd experienced the best that there was, Ethan's clever mouth brought another wave to fruition.

And then another. Until she cried out something unintelligible. Whether she was asking for mercy or for more, neither one of them knew.

But suddenly, there he was, over her, pressing her deep into her bed as he slid his hard body along hers, activating yet another host of sensations until she was completely convinced that she had somehow just vibrated into an alternative universe where pleasure was king and nothing else mattered. Ever.

Breathing hard now, trying vainly to draw in enough air to sustain herself, Kansas parted her legs and opened for him.

And cried out his name as she felt him enter.

The music suddenly materialized in her head, coming from nowhere.

The dance began slowly, building quickly.

A waltz developed into a samba, then the tempo went faster and faster until the final moment with its satisfying dispersion of mind-numbing sensations echoed within them both.

It was like New Year's Eve when the clock struck midnight and confetti came raining down, accompanied by cries of good wishes and happiness.

Gradually, she became aware of clinging to Ethan, became aware that her arms were still wrapped tightly around his back and that her body was still arching into his even though he was on top.

She became aware as well that his breathing was just as short as hers.

And aware, most of all, that she didn't want this very special moment to end. Didn't want to exchange what she was feeling for reality, where guilt and vulnerability and, most of all, disappointment resided, ready to rain on her parade.

But the moment linked itself to another and then another until finally, the descent came, slowly rather than rapidly, but it came. And it brought her down with it.

She felt Ethan shift his weight off her and realized that he'd been propping himself on his elbows the entire time they'd made love to spare her being oppressed by his weight.

That was when she recalled having trouble breathing when Grant made love with her. Grant always allowed his full weight to press against her, against her lungs, after he'd satisfied himself. Once he'd actually fallen asleep and had gotten angry at her for waking him up. He claimed not to remember the incident when he was awake the next day. And because she loved him, because she wanted him to love her, she'd believed him.

Or said she had.

They weren't the same kind of men at all, he and Ethan, she realized. Maybe there really were two different kinds of men. The good ones and the bad ones.

*No, don't do that. Don't go there,* she warned herself sternly. *You're just going to start hoping and setting yourself up for a fall. You fell once, crashing and burning, remember? That should be enough for anyone, including you.*

She felt Ethan's smile before she saw it.

Turning her head to look at him, Kansas saw that she was right. He was smiling. Grinning, really. Was he laughing at her, enjoying some private joke at her expense?

She could feel herself withdrawing. "What?" she demanded.

His smile seem to soften, or maybe that was wishful thinking on her part, a way for her to save face in her own eyes.

"You, Kansas," he told her, "are just full of surprises."

She could feel her defenses going up, and just like that, she was ready for a fight. "Meaning?"

"Meaning I don't think I've ever actually been blown away before." He stopped as if he was thinking, trying to remember. But there was no need to think, really. Because he already knew. "No, never blown away. Until now." He combed his fingers through her hair, looking into her eyes. Despite everything, all those defenses she thought she'd just hastily thrown up, she felt herself melting. "You really can make the earth move, can't you?"

What she wanted to do was lean into his touch. But she knew the danger in that. Instead, she rebuffed his words. "You don't have to flatter me, O'Brien. We already made love," she pointed out.

"I don't *have* to do anything at all," he told her. "I tend not to, as a matter of fact. Kyle's the family rebel, but that doesn't mean that Greer and I just fall docilely into step, doing whatever we're told, following all the rules just because they're rules." His smile deepened as he looked at her, thoughts cropping up in his head that he was not willing to share yet—if ever. "You, Beckett, are a force to be reckoned with. But I already kind of figured you would be."

He was doing it again, she thought, he was breaching her soul. But somehow the sense of alarm that should have accompanied that realization was missing. "Oh, you did, did you?"

He traced a light, circular pattern along the back of her neck and managed to send shivers down her spine. "Yup."

"Is that because you think you're such a red-hot lover?" she asked, doing her best to sound sarcastic. But her heart just wasn't in it. Her heart was elsewhere. Hoping…

"No," he answered seriously, his eyes holding hers. "It's because I'm a pretty good judge of people."

"And does this ability to correctly judge people help you guess what's going to come next?"

"Sometimes," he allowed.

"Okay," she challenged, "what's going to come next now?"

She could feel his smile getting under her skin as it spread over his lips. "Surprise me," he whispered.

Funny how a whisper could send such shock waves through her system, she thought. "That," she informed him as a sexy smile curved her lips, "is a downright dangerous challenge."

"Oh God, I certainly hope so."

Then, before she could comment on his response, Ethan pulled her to him, his mouth covering hers. Silencing her the best way he knew how.

It was the best way she knew how…as well.

## Chapter 13

There had to be something. *Something,* Kansas insisted silently as she sat at the desk that, after more than a month of being here, she'd begun to regard as her own. She felt as if she'd been reexamining files forever.

It was late and everyone on the task force had gone home long ago. She'd even sent away Ethan, who had remained after the others—including the two extra detectives the chief had given them—had left, trying to do what he could to make the tedious process go faster. But another case he'd been working on had required his attention as well, and consequently he'd gotten next to no sleep in over two days.

He was beginning to resemble death walking, she'd told him, insisting that he go home. Ethan had finally given in about ninety minutes ago, leaving the precinct after making her promise that she'd only remain another few minutes.

A "few minutes" had knitted themselves into an hour, and then more. She was still here.

But there was nothing waiting for her at home, and she felt far too wired to actually get any sleep, so she reasoned that she might as well stay and work. At least if she was working, she wouldn't be tempted to call Ethan, suggesting a really late dinner. That was, at best, thinly veiled code for what she knew would happen.

It wasn't the thought of dinner that aroused her. It was the thought of sitting opposite Ethan in a setting where she didn't have to remain the consummate professional. Where, mentally, she would count off the minutes before he would reach for her and they would make love again.

After that first night together, there had been several more evenings that had ended with their clothes being left in a heap on the floor and their bodies gloriously entwined.

And with each time that they made love, she found that instead of finally becoming sated, she just wanted more.

Always more.

At least if she was here, embroiled in what was beginning to look like a futile hunt, she couldn't do anything about getting together with Ethan. Superman or not, the man did need his sleep.

As for her, Kansas thought, she needed to be vindicated, to prove to herself that she hadn't all but destroyed her hard-won career with the fire department on a baseless hunch.

She was right, Kansas silently insisted. She could feel it in her bones. She just needed to find something, that one elusive, tiny trace of something or other that would finally lead her to the person who was responsible for setting the fires.

But so far, it didn't look as if she was going to get anywhere. All the firefighters who had responded to the various alarms seemed to be above reproach. There were no citations, no disciplinary actions of any kind in their personal files.

The only unusual notation that she'd come across was the one in Nathan Bonner's folder. He was the firefighter who had come on the job after she was no longer an active member of the team. The captain had inserted a handwritten note that said the man was almost too eager, too ready to give 110 percent each and every time. The captain was afraid he was going to burn himself out before his time. Otherwise, he was excellent.

She sighed, leaning back in her chair, staring at the screen and the database that she'd been using. Her methodical review had been eliminating suspects one by one until, instead of at least a few left standing, there was no one. From all indications, this was a sterling group of men.

They probably didn't even cheat on their taxes, she thought, disgruntled. Too bad. When all else failed, the authorities caught racketeers and career criminals by scrutinizing their taxes. Income tax evasion was the way the FBI had brought down the infamous Al Capone. Her mouth curved at the irony in that. When in doubt, check out their tax forms.

She sat up, straight as an arrow, as the thought registered.

Why not?

She'd tried every other avenue. Maybe she *could* find something in their income tax forms that she could use. At this point, Kansas was desperate enough to try anything.

Pressing her lips together, she stared at the screen, thinking. Trying her best to remember. When she was in college, before she'd thought that the world began and ended with Grant, she'd gone out with a Joe Balanchine. Joe had an ingrained knack for making computers do whatever he needed them to do. Trying to impress her, he'd taught her a few things, like how easy it was to hack into files that were supposedly beyond hacking.

"Here's hoping I can remember what you taught me, Joe," she murmured.

It took her several unsuccessful tries before she finally managed to scale the electronic cyberspace walls and hack into the system. When it finally opened up, allowing her to access federal and state income tax data, Kansas felt almost giddy with triumph.

She realized that she should have taken that as a sign that maybe it was time for her to go home and get some sleep, approaching this from a fresh perspective tomorrow morning. But again, she was far too wired to even contemplate going to bed. If she went home now, she'd spend the night staring at the ceiling.

Or calling Ethan.

The latter thought had her chewing on her lower lip. When had that become the norm for her? When had sharing moments large and small with Ethan become something she looked forward to? This was dangerous ground she was traversing, and she knew it.

But right now, she was far too happy with this latest success to care.

With the firefighters' Social Security numbers at her fingertips, she arranged them in ascending numerical order. That done, she quickly went from one file to another, using the seven-year window that had once been the standard number of years an audit could go back and hold the taxpayer culpable for any errors, unintentional or not.

Employing a general overview, she went from one firefighter's file to another.

And one by one, she struck out.

She couldn't find a single suspicious notation, a single red flag that an auditor had questioned. There weren't even any random audits.

The euphoria she'd previously experienced faded as dejection took hold. Her eyes swept over the tax forms of the second-to-last firefighter, the numbers hardly penetrating.

This had been her last hope. Her last...

"Hello," she murmured to herself, sitting up. "What's this?"

Blinking a few times to make sure she wasn't seeing something that wasn't there—or rather, not seeing something that was, she focused on Nathan Bonner's file.

"So you *do* have a skeleton in your closet," she said to the screen, addressing it as if she were talking to Bonner. The likeable firefighter's returns went back only three years. The same amount of time he'd been with the Aurora Fire Department.

According to the form he'd filled out when he joined

the department, he had transferred from a firehouse in Providence, Rhode Island. She recalled seeing copies of glowing letters of recommendation in his file. But if that were the case, he would have had to have worked at the firehouse there. And earned a living. Which necessitated filing a tax form.

And he hadn't.

Kansas went through the records a second time. And then a third. There were no returns filed from that period.

Maybe it wasn't Rhode Island. Maybe it was somewhere else. She did a search, using just his name and inputting it into each state, one by one. A Nathan Bonner, with his Social Security number, finally turned up in New York City. With a death certificate.

She sat back, staring at the information. Nathan Bonner died in a car accident in January of 2001. He was seventy-five years old at the time. The Social Security number and month and date of birth all matched the ones that Bonner had claimed were his.

Wow.

"Nathan Bonner" was a fraud, she thought, her heart launching into double time. This was it, this was what she was looking for. Bonner was their firebug. He had to be. She didn't know why he'd gone through this elaborate charade or what else he was up to, but he was their man. She was sure of it.

Excited, she grabbed the phone receiver and was inputting Ethan's cell-phone number. He had to hear this.

The phone on the other end rang four times and then Kansas heard it being picked up. She was almost breathless as she started talking. "Ethan, it's Kansas. Listen, I think that—"

"You've reached Ethan O'Brien's cell phone. I can't talk right now, but if you leave your—"

"Damn it!" Impatience ate away at Kansas. Was he sound asleep? She heard the tone ring in her ear. "Ethan, it's Kansas. If you get this message, call me. I think I found our man." Why hadn't she gotten the number of his landline? At least when she left a message, if he was anywhere in the area, she stood a good chance of waking him up by talking loudly.

Biting off an oath, she hung up.

She contemplated her next move. Everyone liked Bonner. He was friendly and outgoing and appeared to take an interest in everyone around him. He was always willing to listen, always willing to go catch a beer at the end of the day—or lend money to tide a brother firefighter over to the next paycheck.

If she suggested that he was behind the fires, the rest of the house would demand her head on a platter. There was no way anyone was going to believe her without proof.

Okay, if it's proof they wanted, proof they were going to get. She hit the print button, printing everything she'd just read. She'd need it to back her up.

Once that was done and she had collected the pages from the mouth of the printer, she tried calling Ethan again. With the same results. She hung up just before his voice mail picked up.

Frustrated, she deposited the papers she'd just printed into a folder. She wanted Ethan to see this. The sooner the better. He was, as he'd claimed, her partner, and he needed to see proof that she was right. That he hadn't just backed her up only to have her take a dive off a cliff.

Humming, she got her things together and left the squad room.

She barely remembered the trip to Ethan's apartment. She'd been there only twice before. Once to return his cell phone that first night—and once when he'd brought her to his place after taking her out for dinner and a movie.

Her mouth curved. Just like two normal people. That night they'd made love until they fell asleep, exhausted, in each other's arms.

Excitement raced through her veins, and it was hard to say what was more responsible for her getting to that state—the fact that she was convinced that she'd found their firebug or that she was going to Ethan's apartment to see him.

By her calculation, Ethan had gotten about two hours' sleep if he'd gone right home and straight to bed. A person could go far on two hours if he had to, she reasoned. God knew she had. More than once.

And she *knew* Ethan wouldn't want her to wait until morning with this.

Pulling up directly in front of his apartment, taking a slot that she knew had to belong to someone else who, conveniently, was gone at the moment, she jumped out of her car. She didn't even bother locking the doors. She'd move the car later, but right now she had to see him.

Kansas headed straight for his door. It took everything she had to keep from pounding on it. Instead, she just knocked on his door as if this were nothing more than just a social visit instead of one that ultimately was a matter of life and death. They needed to catch Bonner before he set off another device.

When no one answered her knock, she knocked again, harder this time. Hard enough to hurt her knuckles.

"C'mon, c'mon. Wake up, Ethan," she called, raising her voice and hoping that it carried through the door. Just as she was about to try to call him on her cell again, thinking that the combination of pounding and ringing phone would finally wake him, the door to his apartment opened.

"Well, it's about time that yo—"

The rest of the sentence froze on her tongue. She wasn't looking at Ethan. She was looking at a woman. A gorgeous blonde with hypnotic eyes.

She felt as if someone had punched her in the stomach. Just the way she'd felt when she'd walked in on Grant and the hotel receptionist.

Stunned speechless, Kansas took a step back. "I'm sorry, I must have made—"

That was when she saw Ethan approaching from the rear of the apartment. Where the bedroom was located. He was barefoot and wearing the bottom half of a pair of navy blue pajamas. The ones he kept at the foot of his bed in case he had to throw something on to answer the door at night, he'd told her.

"—a mistake," she concluded. "I've made a terrible mistake. I'm sorry to have bothered you," she told the woman coldly. Kansas turned on her heel and hurried away, leaving the woman in the doorway looking after her, confused.

She heard Ethan call her name, but she refused to stop, refused to turn around. She was too angry. At him. At herself.

And too full of pain.

Damn it, it had happened again. She'd *let* it happen again. How could she have been naive enough, stupid enough to think that Ethan was different? That he could actually be someone who was faithful? It was inherently against a man's religion to be faithful, and she should have her head examined for thinking it was remotely possible.

Getting into the car, she didn't even bother securing her seat belt. She just started the car and put it into Drive.

Kansas felt her eyes stinging and she blinked several times, trying to push back her tears, fiercely telling herself that she wasn't going to cry. He wasn't worth tears.

*No strings, remember? You promised yourself no strings. Strings just trip you up,* she told herself. *What the hell happened?*

"Kansas, stop!" Ethan called after her.

She deliberately shut his voice out. All she wanted to do was get away.

*Now.*

She should have never come here—no, she amended, she *should* have. Otherwise, how would she have ever found out that he was just like all the rest? Deceitful and a cheat. Better now than later when she—

Kansas swallowed a scream. Keen reflexes had her swerving to the left at the last minute to avoid hitting him. Ethan had raced after her and had managed, via some shortcut he must have taken, to get right in front of her. He had his hand on her hood in an instant, using himself as a human roadblock.

Her heart pounded so wildly it was hurting her chest. Had she gone an instant quicker, been driving an instant faster, she wouldn't have been able to swerve away in time.

Angry as she was at him, she didn't want to think about that.

Had it not been so late, she would have leaned on her horn. Instead, she rolled down her window and shouted, "Get out of the way."

"Not until you tell me what's wrong with you," he ground out between teeth that were clenched together to keep from giving her a piece of his mind.

"Nothing anymore," she declared, lifting her chin in what he'd come to know as sheer defiance. "Now get the hell out of the way or I'll run you over. I swear I will," she threatened.

A movement in her rearview mirror caught her eye. The woman who'd opened the door was hurrying toward them. Great, that was all she needed. To see the two of them together.

"Your girlfriend's coming," she informed him, icicles clinging to every syllable. "Go and talk to her."

"What the hell are you talking about?" Ethan demanded. "What girlfriend?"

Did he think that if he denied any involvement, she'd fall into his arms like a newly returned puppy? "The one who opened the door."

He looked at her as if he was trying to decide if she'd

lost her mind—or he had. Glancing behind the car for confirmation, he told her, "That's Greer."

Was that supposed to make her feel as if they were all friends? "I don't care what her name is. Just go to her and get out of my way." She gripped the steering wheel as if she intended to go, one way or another.

The woman he'd just referred to as Greer peered into the passenger-side window. In contrast to Ethan, she looked calm and serene. And she had the audacity to smile at her.

The next moment, she was extending her hand to her through the opened window. "Hi, we haven't met yet. I'm Greer. Ethan's sister."

Had her whole body not been rigid with tension, her jaw would have dropped in her lap. "His what?"

"Sister," Ethan repeated for her benefit. "I told you I had one."

A sense of embarrassment was beginning to shimmer just on the perimeter of her consciousness. She valiantly held it at bay, but the feeling of having acted like a fool was blowing holes in her shield.

"You said you were triplets," Kansas protested. "She's a blonde. She doesn't look like you—"

"And I thank God every day for that," Greer interjected with a very wide grin. A grin that made her resemble Ethan, Kansas thought, chagrined. "I'm going to go, Ethan. Thanks for the pep talk, I really appreciate it." She looked from the woman behind the wheel to her barefoot brother. "I didn't mean to wake you," she apologized. About to walk away, she stopped and added, "By the way, you're right," she told her brother, amusement in her eyes. "She really is something."

And then she nodded at her. "Hope to see you again, Kansas."

For a second, Kansas was silent, watching the other woman walk to her car. "She knows my name?" she asked Ethan.

"Yeah." His expression gave nothing away.

There was only one reason for that as far as Kansas knew. "You told her about me."

Ethan shrugged carelessly. "Your name might have come up." And then a smattering of anger returned. "What the hell is all this about?" he wanted to know.

As embarrassing and revealing as it was, Kansas told him the truth. She owed him that much for having acted the way she had. But it wasn't easy. Baring her soul never was.

"For a minute, I thought I was reliving a scene from my past," she confessed.

His eyes narrowed. "Involving your husband, the idiot?"

Kansas pressed her lips together before nodding. "Yes."

"I'm not him, Kansas." He wondered if he would ever get that through to her. And what it would do to their relationship if he couldn't.

It wasn't in her nature to say she was sorry. For the first time, she caught herself wishing that it was. But the words wouldn't come no matter how much she willed them to. Saying "I know" was the best she could do.

"Good. Now go park your car and come back inside." He looked down at the pajama bottoms. "I'm going to go in before someone calls the police to complain about a half-naked man running around in the parking lot, playing dodgeball with a car."

The moon was out and rays of moonlight seemed to highlight the definition of his muscles. The term "magnificent beast" came to mind. "I don't think they'd be complaining if they actually saw you," she told him.

His eyes met hers. Again, she couldn't tell what he was thinking—or feeling. "It's going to take more than a few words of flattery to make up for this."

"Maybe when you hear why I came in the first place, you'll find it in your heart to forgive me." Mentally, she crossed her fingers.

"We'll see," he told her, making no promises one way or another.

Turning away, Ethan hiked up the pajama bottoms that were resting precariously on his hip bone, threatening to slip, and started back to his apartment.

Kansas sat in her car, watching him walk away, appreciating the view and trying not to let her imagination carry her away.

It was a couple of minutes before Kansas started up her car engine again. Her other engine was already revving.

## Chapter 14

"Do you really think that little of me?" Ethan demanded, his voice controlled, the second she walked in. "So little that you just assume that if I'm with another woman, it has to be something sexual? That I have to be cheating on you?"

"No, I don't think that little of you," she answered, raising her voice to get him to stop talking for a moment and listen. "I think that little of *me*." He looked at her, confused, so she elaborated. "I'm not exactly the greatest judge of character when it comes to the men in my personal life. I try not to have a personal life because… because…" The words stuck in her throat and her voice trailed off.

"Because you're afraid of making a mistake?" he guessed.

She shrugged dismissively, wanting to be done with

this line of discussion, and looked away. "Something like that."

Ethan threaded his fingers through her hair, framing her face with his palms and gently forcing her to look at him. When she did, he brought his mouth down to hers and kissed her with bone-melting intensity.

After a very long moment, he drew back and asked her, "Does that feel like a mistake?"

Kansas's adrenaline had already launched into double time, threatening to go into triple. Everything else was put on hold, or temporarily forgotten.

The only thing that mattered was experiencing heaven one more time.

At least one more time, she silently pleaded with whoever might be listening. Because tomorrow would come and it might not be kind. But she had today, she had right now, and she desperately wanted to make the most of it.

"Ask me again later," she breathed. "I'm too busy now."

And with that, she recaptured his lips with her own and slipped off for another dip in paradise's sun-kissed waters.

He lost no time in joining her.

It wasn't until dawn the next morning, as Kansas woke up by degrees in his arms and slowly started removing the cobwebs from her brain, that she began thinking clearly again.

"What was it that you came here to tell me?" Ethan wanted to know, bringing everything back into focus for her.

Kansas raised herself up on her elbow to look at this man who, however unintentionally, kept rocking her world. From his expression, he'd been watching her sleep again. The fact that he hadn't woken her up with this question, that he'd waited until she'd opened her eyes on her own, just reinforced what she already knew to be true—the man was completely devoid of any curiosity.

Unlike her.

She needed to know everything. Public things, private things, it made absolutely no difference. She had always had this incredibly insatiable desire to know everything.

As for him, if the information wouldn't help him crack a case, he could wait it out—or even have it just fade away. It appeared to be all one and the same to Ethan.

"It's about Nathan Bonner—" She saw that there was no immediate recognition evident in his expression when she said the name. "The firefighter who was giving that old man from the nursing home CPR. The old man who died," she added.

It was the last piece that had the light dawning in his eyes.

"Oh him, right."

Playing with a strand of her hair, he was completely amazed that he could be so fiercely drawn to a woman. In the past, his usual MO was to make love with someone a couple of times—three, tops—and then move on, deliberately shunning any strings. But he didn't want to move on this time. He wanted to dig in for the long haul.

*That* had never happened to him before.

"What about him?" Ethan asked, whispering the question into her hair.

His breath warmed her scalp and sent ripples throughout her being. If this wasn't so important, she would have just given in to the feeling and made love with him. It was a hell of a good way to start the day.

But this had to be said. Ethan needed to know what she had discovered. "He doesn't exist."

Ethan looked at her, somewhat confused. "Come again?"

"Nathan Bonner doesn't exist," Kansas told him, enunciating each word slowly—then quickly explaining how she'd come to her conclusion. "He didn't even exist seven years ago. There're no federal income tax forms filed except for the last three years. If you go back four, there's nothing. No driver's license, no tax forms, no credit cards. Nothing," she emphasized.

Ethan stopped curling her hair around his finger and straightened, as if put on some kind of alert. Kansas had managed to get his undivided attention. "Hold it. Just how did you get hold of his tax records?"

A protective feeling nudged forward within her. Kansas shook her head, even though she knew her response frustrated him. She couldn't tell him how she'd gotten the information.

"If I don't tell you, the chief can't blame you," she told him. "Or kill you." Then, because he was staring at her intently, obviously not pleased with her answer, she sighed. It wasn't that she didn't trust him. She didn't want him blamed. But he had to know that her information was on the level. "I hacked into his files. His and a few others," she confessed.

For a second, she looked away and heard him ask in a quiet voice, "How many are a few?"

She thought of hedging, then decided against it. "All of them," she said quietly.

He'd never been this close to speechless before. "Kansas—"

"I was looking for something we could use," she explained, afraid he was going to launch into a lecture. "I didn't expect to find that Bonner was just an alias this guy was using." The moment he disappeared off the grid, she started hunting through old tax returns, trying to match the Social Security number. Her dogged efforts brought success. "He got his identity off a dead man."

That kind of thing happened in the movies, not real life. Ethan cast about for a reasonable explanation. "Maybe he's in the witness protection program."

The suggestion took some of the wind out of her sails.

"I suppose that could be one possibility." She rolled the idea over in her mind. Her gut told her it was wrong, but she knew she was going to need more than her gut to nail this down. "Do you know anyone in the marshal's office?" she asked him. "Someone who could check this out for us?"

Ethan grinned in response. She was obviously forgetting who she was talking to. "I'm a Cavanaugh by proxy. If I can't find out, someone within the family unit can."

There were definite advantages to having a large family beyond the very obvious, she thought with a mild touch of envy. "You're going to need a search warrant," she added.

"*We* are going to need a search warrant," he corrected.

"No," she contradicted him in a deceptively mild voice that made him decidedly uneasy. "Technically I can search his place, warrant or no warrant. Some people might see that as breaking and entering, but if I find anything incriminating, it *can* be used against him."

Ethan knew that look by now. It was the one that all but screamed "reckless." He had a feeling that it was probably useless, but he had to say this anyway. "Don't do anything stupid, Kansas."

The expression she gave him was innocence personified. "I never do anything stupid."

It took all he had not to laugh. "I wouldn't put that up for a vote if I were you." Throwing back the covers, he got up and then held his hand out to her. "C'mon, let's shower."

Taking it, she swung her legs out to the side and rose. "Together?"

Ethan paused for a second just to drink in the sight. Damn, he wanted her more each time he was with her. "It'll save time," he promised.

But it didn't.

Within an hour, they were at the firehouse. Together they confronted the captain with their request.

The veneer on the spirit of cooperation had worn thin and there was definite hostility in Captain Lawrence's eyes as he regarded them. The brunt of it was directed at Kansas.

"Bonner? You've already questioned everyone here once. Why do you want to talk to him again?" Lawrence demanded impatiently. The question was underscored with a glare. Before either could answer, the captain said, "He's one of the best firefighters I've ever had the privilege of working with. I don't want you harassing him."

Ethan took the lead, trying once again to divert the captain's anger onto him instead of Kansas. After all, she had to come back here and work with the man as well as the other firefighters. A situation, he thought, that was looking more and more bleak as time wore on.

"We just want to ask him a few more questions, Captain. Like why there's no record of him before he came to the firehouse. And why he has the same Social Security number as a guy who died in 2001."

If this new information stunned him, the captain gave no such indication. He merely shrugged it off. "That's gotta be a mistake of some sort," he replied firmly. "You know what record keeping is like with the government."

"Maybe," Ethan allowed. "But that's why we want to talk to Bonner, to clear up any misunderstanding."

"Well, you're out of luck." Lawrence began to walk to his small, cluttered office. "I insisted he take the day off. He'd been on duty for close to three weeks straight. The man's like a machine. We've been short-handed this last month, and he's been filling in for one guy after another."

"Isn't that unusual?" Ethan challenged. "To have a firefighter on duty for that long?"

"That's just the kind of guy he is," the captain pointed out proudly. "I wish I had a firehouse full of Bonners."

"No, you don't," Kansas said under her breath as Ethan asked the man for Bonner's home address.

The look that the older man slanted toward her told Kansas that her voice hadn't been as quiet as she'd initially thought.

Less than twenty minutes later they were walking up to Bonner's door. The man without an identity lived in a residential area located not too far from the firehouse where he worked. The ride to work probably took him a matter of minutes.

Ethan rang the doorbell. It took several attempts to get Bonner to answer his front door.

When the firefighter saw who was on his doorstep, the warm, friendly smile on his lips only grew more so. Kansas would have wavered in her convictions had she not read the files herself. The man looked like the personification of geniality.

"Sorry," he apologized. "I was just catching up on some Z's. I like to do that on my day off. It recharges my batteries," he explained. "Come on in." Opening the door all the way to admit them, he stepped to the side. "Sorry about the place being such a mess, but I've been kind of busy, doing double shifts at the firehouse. We're short a couple of guys, and since I really don't have anything special on my agenda, I volunteered to pick up the slack. The pay's good," he confided, "but it leaves my house looking like a tornado hit it."

"I've seen worse," Kansas told him as she looked around.

Actually, she thought, she'd lived in worse. One of the foster mothers who had taken her in, Mrs. Novak, had an obsessive-compulsive disorder that wouldn't allow her to throw anything out. Eventually, social services came to remove her from the home because of the health hazards that living there presented.

But for all her quirkiness, Mrs. Novak had been kinder to her than most of the other foster mothers she had lived with. Those women had taken her in strictly because she represented monthly checks from social services. Mrs. Novak was lonely and wanted someone to talk to.

"What can I do for you?" the firefighter asked cheerfully.

"You can tell us why you're using a dead man's Social Security number," Kansas demanded, beating Ethan to the punch. She slanted a quick glance in his direction and saw him shaking his head. At any other time, she might have thought that her partner looked displeased because she had stolen his thunder. But not in this case. Ethan wasn't like that. He wasn't, she had to admit, like any of the other men she'd worked with. Maybe he thought she should have worded her statement more carefully.

*Too late now.*

"Oh." The firefighter cleared his throat, looking just a tad uncomfortable. "That."

The response surprised Kansas. Her eyes widened

as she exchanged a glance with Ethan. Was Bonner, or whatever his name was, actually admitting to his deception? It couldn't be this easy.

"Do you care to explain?'" Ethan prodded, giving him a chance to state his side.

The firefighter took a breath before starting. "All my life I wanted to be a fireman. I was afraid if they saw my record, they wouldn't let me join."

"Record?" Ethan asked. Just what kind of a record was the man talking about? Was he a wanted criminal?

"Oh, nothing serious," the firefighter quickly reassured them. "I just got into trouble a couple of time as a teenager." In his next breath, he dismissed the infractions. "Typical kid pranks. One of my friends took his uncle's car for a joyride. I went along with a couple of other guys. But he didn't tell his uncle he was taking it, so his uncle reported the car stolen and, you guessed it, we were all picked up.

"I tried to explain that I hadn't known that Alvin was driving without his uncle's blessings, and the policeman I was talking to thought I was giving him attitude." He shrugged. "He tried to use his nightstick, and I wouldn't let him hit me with it. I was defending myself, but the judge in juvenile court called it assaulting an officer of the law." And then he raised his hand as if he were taking a solemn oath. "But that's the sum total of my record, I swear on my mother's eyes."

Ethan supposed that could be true, but then, since it could all be explained away, why had he gone through this elaborate charade?

"That doesn't exactly make you sound like a hardened criminal," Ethan pointed out.

Bonner looked chagrined. "I know, I know, but I was afraid to risk it. I didn't want to throw away the dream."

"Of rushing into burning buildings," Ethan concluded incredulously. Most people he knew didn't dream about taking risks like that.

"Of saving lives," the other man countered, his voice and demeanor solemn.

That seemed to do it for Ethan. He rose to his feet and shook the firefighter's hand. "Sorry to have bothered you, Mr. Bonner."

Ethan glanced at Kansas. She had no choice but to rise to her feet as well, no matter what her gut was currently screaming.

A bright smile flashed across the firefighter's lips. "No bother at all," Nathan assured him. He walked them to the front door. "I understand. It's your job to check these things out. In your place, I would have done the same thing. That's why this city gets such high marks for safety year after year," he said, opening the door for them.

The minute they were alone, as they walked to his car, Ethan said to Kansas, "It all sounds plausible." Before she had a chance to comment, his cell phone began ringing. Taking it out of his pocket, he flipped it open. "O'Brien. Oh, hi, Janelle. How's that search warrant coming?" He frowned. "It's not? Why?" He said the word just as Kansas fired it at him in frustrated bewilderment. His response was to turn away from her so he wouldn't be distracted. "Uh-huh. I see. Okay. Well, you tried. I appreciate it, Janelle. Thanks anyway." With that, he terminated the call.

Kansas was filling in the blanks. "No search warrant?"

He nodded, shoving the phone back into his pocket. They were at the curb and he released the locks on the car's doors. "That's what the lady said. Turns out the judge that Janelle approached for the search warrant had his house saved from burning to the ground last year by guess who."

Kansas sighed. "Bonner."

He gestured like a game show host toward the winning contestant after the right answer had been given. "Give the lady a cigar."

She opened the passenger-side door and got in. "The lady would rather have a search warrant."

"Maybe we can find another way to get it," he told her, although he didn't hold out much hope for that. "But maybe," Ethan continued, knowing she didn't want to hear this, "it's as simple as what Bonner or whoever he really is said. He didn't want to risk not being allowed to become a firefighter because he was a stupid kid who went joyriding with the wrong people."

Kansas stared off into space. "Maybe," she repeated. But he knew that she didn't believe that for a moment.

The rest of the day was mired in the same sort of frustrating tedium. Every avenue they followed led nowhere. By the end of the day Kansas was far more exhausted mentally than physically. So much so that she felt as if she were going to self-combust, she told Ethan as he parked his car in her apartment complex.

Ethan grinned seductively. Getting out of his beloved

Thunderbird, he came around to her side of the car and opened the door.

"I have just the remedy for that," he promised, taking her hand and drawing her toward the door.

She hardly heard him. "Maybe if I just go over—"

He cut her off. "You've gone over everything at least twice if not three times. Anything you come up with now can keep until morning. Right now," he whispered into her ear, "I just want to get you into your apartment and get you naked."

That did have promise, she mused, her blood already heating. "I take it your girlfriend canceled on you," she deadpanned.

"Don't have a girlfriend," he told her, and then added, "Other than you," so seriously that it took her breath away.

"Is that what I am?" she heard herself asking, her throat suddenly extra dry. All the while a little voice kept warning her not to get carried away, not to let down all her barriers because that left her far too vulnerable. And she knew what happened when she was too vulnerable. Her heart suffered for it.

"Well, you're certainly not my boyfriend," he answered, his eyes washing over her warmly.

"I don't think they really use that word anymore," she told him. "Girlfriend," she repeated in case he didn't understand which word she was referring to.

"I don't really plan to use any words, either—once I get you behind closed doors."

He saw what he took to be hesitation in her eyes and gave it his own interpretation. She was thinking about the case, he guessed. It was going to consume her if he didn't do something about it.

"It's the best way I know of to unwind," Ethan assured her. "Do it for the job," he coaxed. When she looked at him in confusion, he explained, "This way, you'll be able to start fresh in the morning. Maybe even find that angle you've been looking for."

The man could sell hair dryers to a colony of bald people. "Well, if you put it that way…you talked me into it."

Slipping his arm around her waist, he pulled her to him. "I had a hunch I would."

# Chapter 15

Kansas couldn't let go of the idea that she was right, that Bonner, or whatever his real name was, was the one who was behind the fires.

For a while, as Ethan made love to her, she hadn't a thought in her head—other than she loved being with this man and making love with him.

But now that he was lying beside her, sound asleep, she'd begun to think again.

And focus.

And maybe, she silently admitted, to obsess.

She just couldn't let go of the idea that she was dead-on about Nathan Bonner. Furthermore, she was afraid that he had a large, packed suitcase somewhere, one he could grab at a moment's notice and flee.

If he hadn't already.

She desperately wanted to look around his house, and, more important, to look around his garage. If she were part of the police force, the way Ethan was, her hands would be tied until that search warrant materialized—and that might never happen.

But she wasn't part of the police force, she thought, becoming steadily more motivated to take action. She was part of the fire department—a situation she had more than a sneaking suspicion might not be the case very soon. But right now she was still a fire investigator. And as such, she could very easily look around, turning things over to the police if she found anything the least bit incriminating. It was her job to prevent fires from starting.

Granted, entering Bonner's garage was technically, as she'd said to Ethan, breaking and entering, but if she found what she thought she would find, she sincerely doubted that she'd be charged with anything.

Even if she was, it would be worth it if she could stop this man from setting even one more fire.

Very slowly, moving an inch at a time so as not to wake Ethan, she slipped out of bed. Once her feet were finally on the floor, she quickly gathered up her scattered clothes and snuck out of the room.

Entering the living room, she left the light off and hurried into her clothing. With her purse in one hand and her shoes in another, she quietly opened the front door and eased herself out. Closing the door behind her took an equally long amount of time. The last thing she wanted to do was wake Ethan up. She knew that he would immediately ask where she was going.

She couldn't tell him the truth because he would stop her, and she didn't want to lie to him. Sneaking out like this allowed her to avoid either scenario.

Kansas quickly put together a course of action in her head while driving to the house of the man she now regarded as the firebug. She couldn't very well knock on his door and ask to see his garage. He was within his rights to refuse.

Her only option was not to give him that opportunity.

She'd noticed, as she and Ethan had left the man's house, that the garage had a side entrance as well as the standard garage doors that opened and closed by remote control.

Her way in was the side door.

More than likely, the door was locked, but that didn't pose a deterrent. Picking a lock was exceedingly simple if you knew what you were doing. And she, thanks to one of the foster kids whose path had crossed hers, did.

Because there was no traffic in the middle of the night, she arrived at her destination fairly quickly. Parking her vehicle more than half a block away from Bonner's house, Kansas made her way over to the one-story stucco building, keeping well to the shadows whenever possible.

Bonner, she noted, wasn't one of those people who left his front porch lights on all night. The lights were off. That worked in her favor, she thought, relieved.

Within a minute and a half of accessing the garage's side door, she'd picked the padlock and was inside the structure.

Taking out a pencil-thin, high-powered flashlight, Kansas illuminated the area directly in front of her.

She was extra careful not to trip over anything or send something clattering to the finished stone floor.

There was no car inside the garage, no car outside in the driveway, either. Maybe he was gone, or on call, she thought. Either way, she still wasn't going to take any chances and turn on the lights.

That, however, did slow down any kind of progress to a crawl. It wasn't easy restraining herself this way, considering the impatience drumming through her veins and the fact that the garage was easily a packrat's idea of heaven. There were boxes and things haphazardly piled up everywhere. Looking around, she sincerely doubted that any vehicle larger than a Smartcar could actually fit in the garage.

Rather than go through the preponderance of boxes, she decided to start with the shelves that lined opposite sides of the structure, methodically going from one floor-to-ceiling array to another.

Twenty minutes in, she got lucky.

Hidden beneath a tarp and tucked away on a bottom shelf situated all the way in the rear of the garage, conveniently behind a tower of boxes, she discovered some very sophisticated incendiary devices.

Several of them.

"Oh my God," she whispered, feeling her insides begin to shake. He wasn't planning on stopping. There were enough devices here for him to go on indefinitely, she realized.

Setting down her flashlight, she angled it for maximum illumination on her find and took out her camera. Holding her breath, Kansas took one photograph after another. This was definitely the proof she needed to convince the captain that he had a rogue firefighter on his hands.

"I'm really sorry you found those, Kansas."

Surprised, she bit down on her lower lip to keep from screaming. She shoved the camera quickly into her pocket before she turned around. When she did, she found herself looking up at Nathan Bonner. His genial expression was gone and he looked far from happy to discover her here.

"You can't do this," she told him. "You can't use these devices. You're liable to kill someone."

He waved away her protest. "No, I won't. I'm an expert on handling these things. Nobody's going to get hurt."

He couldn't believe that, she thought. But, looking into his eyes, she realized that all the dots were not connecting. He had no idea of the kind of havoc that he could bring down on a neighborhood if things went awry. He was too focused on what these fires would accomplish for *him.*

"Like no one was supposed to get hurt at the nursing home?" she challenged.

The firefighter looked genuinely stricken that she should think that he had somehow failed the deceased man. "That was his heart, not the fire."

Was the man that obtuse? "But the fire brought on the heart attack," Kansas cried.

The firefighter didn't seem to hear her. Instead, he grabbed her in what amounted to a bear hug, pinning her arms against her sides. Caught off guard, she desperately tried to get free, doing her best to kick him as hard as she could. But, although she made contact several times, he gave no indication that any of her blows hurt.

"You're going to tire yourself out," he warned. And then he shrugged as he carried her over to an old, dilapidated office chair. It had rusted wheels and its green upholstery was ripped in several places. Each rip bled discolored stuffing. "Maybe it'll be better that way for you."

A cold chill ran down her back. "Why?" Kansas demanded.

"If the fight goes out of you—" he slammed her down onto the chair, and the impact vibrated all the way up through the top of her skull "—you'll go that much quicker."

She thought she picked up a note of regret in his voice, as if he didn't want to do what he was about to do. "You're not talking about letting me go, are you?"

"No, I'm not."

She struggled, straining against the rope that he was wrapping around her as tightly as if it were a cocoon. Using the rope, he secured her to the chair. "I thought you said you planned these things so that no one would get hurt."

"I do. But all those fires have to do with my coming to the rescue. I can't come to your rescue. You made it so I can't come," he told her with a flash of anger just before he applied duct tape over her mouth. "This isn't my fault, you know. It's yours. If you hadn't come around the firehouse, snooping like that—if you hadn't accused me—" his voice grew in volume "—you could have gone on living. And I could have gone on fighting fires. Rescuing people. It's what I'm good at, what I *need* to do." His eyes glinted dangerously. "But you want to spoil everything. I can't let you go now."

For a moment, he stood over her, a towering hulk shaking his head. "You women, you always spoil everything. My mother was like that, always telling me I'd never amount to anything. That I was just some invisible guy that people looked right through. She said no one would ever notice me."

The angry look changed instantly and he beamed. "Well, she was wrong. They notice me, the camera people, they notice me." His hand fisted, he hit the center of his chest proudly. "People are grateful to me. To *me*." And then he sighed, looking down at her. "But I really am sorry it has to be like this."

And then, as she stared, wide-eyed, he was gone, using the side door. She heard him put the padlock back on the door.

He was locking her in.

She'd deal with getting out later, Kansas told herself. Right now, she needed to get untied from this chair. Somewhere along the line, the unbalanced firefighter had learned how to execute some pretty sophisticated knots.

Maybe there was something she could use to cut the ropes on the workbench.

But when she tried to move her chair over, she discovered that the wheels didn't roll. The rust had frozen them in place. She wasn't going anywhere.

Desperate, Kansas began to rock back and forth, increasing the momentum with each pass until she finally got the chair to tip over. The crash jolted through her entire body right down into her teeth. But it also did what she'd hoped. It loosened the ties around her just the slightest bit, giving her enough slack to try to work herself free.

But as she struggled and strained against the ropes, she realized that she smelled something very familiar.

Smoke.

It registered at the same time as the crackling sound of fire eating its way through wood. The entire garage was unfinished, with exposed wood on all four sides. A feast for the fire.

Panic slashed through her.

Kansas forced herself to remain calm. Panic would only have her using up her supply of oxygen faster. Filling her lungs with smoke faster.

*The ropes are loosening,* she told herself. *Stick with the program, Kansas.*

Straining against the ropes, she kept at them relentlessly. The rope cut into her wrists, making them bleed. She couldn't stop, even though she was getting very light-headed and dizzy. Even though her lungs felt as if they were about to burst.

Finally, her eyes stinging, she managed to get one hand partially free. Hunching forward, she bent her head as far as she could. At the same time, she stretched her fingers to the breaking point until she managed to get a little of the duct tape between two of her fingertips. The awkward angle didn't let her pull as hard as she wanted to. But she did what she could.

It seemed as if it was taking forever, but she finally got the tape off her mouth.

She could have cried. Instead, she screamed for help, hoping that someone would hear her. She screamed again, then stopped, afraid that she would wind up swallowing too much smoke if she continued. Using her teeth, she pulled and yanked at the ropes until she got them loose enough to pull her wrist free.

But all this struggling was getting to be too much of an effort for her, all but stealing the oxygen out of her lungs. She was losing ground and she knew it.

Damn it, she wasn't ready to die. Not now, not when it looked as if things might really be going right for her for the first time.

Why had she sneaked out? Why hadn't she told Ethan where she was going? Left him a note, woken him up, something? Anything.

She was going to die and he was never going to know how she felt about him. How she…

Kansas was winking in and out of her head. In and out of consciousness.

The smoke was winning.

She was hallucinating. She thought a car had just come crashing through the garage doors. But that was only wishful thinking. Just like thinking that she heard Ethan's voice, calling her name.

If only…

Her eyes drifted shut.

"Goddamn it, woman, you are a hard person to love," Ethan cried, trying to keep his fears banked down as he raced to her from his beloved Thunderbird, which he'd just embedded in the garage door in an effort to create an opening. He got to her chair-bound body on the floor. There wasn't time to undo her ropes so he lifted her, chair and all, and carried her and it out onto the front lawn.

Just in time.

The next moment, the shingled roof over the garage collapsed, burying the two-car garage in a shower of debris and flames.

Focused only on her, Ethan began cutting her free. Her eyelashes fluttered and then her eyes opened for just a second. His heart leaped into his throat. She was alive!

"Kansas, Kansas, talk to me. Say something. Anything. Please!"

He thought he heard her murmur, "Hi," before she passed out.

When she came around again, she was no longer bound to a chair. Instead, she was strapped to gurney. The gurney was inside an ambulance.

Its back doors gaping open, she could see what was left of Bonner's house. The fire was pretty much out, the embers winking and dying. The fire truck had arrived with its warriors in full regalia, ready to fight yet another fire. It wasn't much of a fight. The fire won before finally retreating into embers.

"Idiot."

Kansas smiled. She could recognize Ethan's voice anywhere.

Turning her head, she saw him sitting beside the gurney. She let the single word pass. "He did it, Ethan. He did it for the attention. He wanted to play the big hero and have everyone say how wonderful he was."

"You were right."

"I was right." She let out a long sigh, exhausted. If

Ethan hadn't come when he had... "How did you know where to find me?"

"Because I know how you think," he told her, torn between being angry at her and just holding her to him to reassure himself that he'd been in time, that she was alive and was going to remain that way. "Like some damn pit bull. Once you get an idea in your head, you don't let go. When I woke up to find you gone, I just *knew* you were at Bonner's house, trying to find something on him any way you could." He looked over at the ashes that had once been a house. "Looks like if there was any evidence, it's gone."

It all came back to her. The fear, the fire and everything that had come before.

"Not necessarily," Kansas told him. He looked at her quizzically. "I took pictures." She touched her pocket to reassure herself that the camera she'd used was still there. It was. "You find him, Ethan, we can convict him. He won't burn anything down anymore." Her voice cracked as it swelled in intensity.

He began to nod his head in agreement, but then he shook it instead. "Never mind about Bonner. I don't care about Bonner." Everything she'd just put him through—the concern, the fear, the horror when he first heard her scream and realized that she was inside the burning garage and he couldn't find a way to get in—came back to him in spades. He could have lost her.

"What the hell were you thinking, coming out here in the middle of the night, poking around an insane man's garage?"

Her throat felt exceedingly dry, but she had to answer him, had to make him understand. "That he had to be stopped. That you couldn't do this because the evidence wouldn't be admissible, but I could because I wasn't bound by the same rules as you were." She stopped for breath. Each word was an effort to get out. Her lungs ached.

He looked at her incredulously, still wanting to shake her even as he wanted to kiss her. "And getting killed never entered you head?"

She smiled that smile of hers, the one that always made him feel as if his kneecaps were made of liquid gelatin. "You know me. I don't think that far ahead."

Meaning she gave no thought to her own safety. He thought of the first night he met her. She'd run into a burning building to rescue children.

Ethan shook his head. "What am I supposed to do with you?"

The kneecap-melting smile turned sexy. "That, Detective, is entirely up to you."

He already had a solution. One he'd been contemplating for the last week. "I suppose I could always put you in protective custody—for the rest of your life."

Had to be the smoke. He couldn't be saying what she thought he was saying. "And just how long do you figure that'll be?"

He took her hand in his, still reassuring himself that she was alive, that he'd gotten to her in time. "Well, if I make sure to watch your every move, maybe the next fifty years."

Okay, it wasn't getting any clearer. "Are you saying what I think you're saying?"

"The way your mind works, I never know," he

admitted. "What is it you think I'm saying?" When she shook her head, unwilling or unable to elaborate, Ethan decided it was time to finally go the whole nine yards and put his feeling into words.

"Okay, maybe I'm not being very clear," he admitted. Leaning in closer so that only she could hear, he said, "I'm asking you to marry me."

A whole host of emotions charged through her like patrons in a theater where someone had just yelled "Fire!" Joy was prominently featured among the emotions, but joy was capped off by fear. Fear because she'd thought herself safe and happy once before, only to watch her world crumble to nothing right in front of her eyes.

She never wanted to be in that position again. "How about we move in together for a while and see how that goes?"

That wasn't the answer he was hoping for. "You don't want to marry me?"

Her first reaction was to shrug away his words, but she owed it to him to be honest more than she owed it to herself to protect herself. "I don't want another broken heart."

"That's not going to happen," he told her with feeling. "You have my word." He held her hand between both of his. "Do you trust me?"

She thought of how he came riding to her rescue—literally. A weak smile curved her mouth. "I guess if I can't trust the word of the man who just messed up the car he loves to save my life, who can I trust? You really sacrificed your car for me," she marveled.

"It doesn't kiss as well as you do," he told her with a straight face.

"Lucky for me."

"Hey, O'Brien." Ortiz stuck his head in, then saw that Kansas was conscious. "How you feeling?" he asked her.

"Like a truck ran over me, but I'll live," she answered.

The detective grinned and nodded his approval. "Good." Then he got back to what he wanted to say to Ethan. "We caught him," he announced triumphantly. "Dispatch just called to say that Bonner was picked up at the Amtrak station, trying to buy a ticket to Sedona. Seems that the machine rejected his credit card." He was looking directly at Ethan when he said the last part.

By the look on Ethan's face, Kansas knew he had to have something to do with the credit card being rejected. "Just how long was I out?"

Ortiz withdrew and Ethan turned his attention back to her. "Long enough for me to get really worried."

"You were worried about me?" She couldn't remember the last time anyone cared enough to be worried about her. It was a good feeling.

This was going to take some time, he thought. But that was all right. He had time. Plenty of time. As long as he could spend it with her. "I tend to worry about the people I love."

She struggled to sit up, leaning on her elbows. "Wait, say that again."

"Which part?" he asked innocently. "'I tend'?"

"No, the other part."

"'…to worry about'?"

She had enough leverage available to be able to hit his arm. "The last part."

"Oh, you mean 'love'?" he asked, watching her face.

"The people I love," she repeated, her teeth gritted together.

"Oh?" He looked at her as if this were all new to him. "And who are these people that you love?"

Why was he toying with her? "Not me. You!" she cried, exasperated.

"You love me?" Ethan asked, looking at her in surprise and amazement.

"Of course I love you—I mean—" And then it hit her. "Wait, you tricked me."

He saw no point in carrying on the little performance any longer. His grin went from ear to ear. "Whatever it takes to get the job done."

She was feeling better. *Much* better. "Oh, just shut up and kiss me."

This he could do. Easily. Taking hold of her shoulders to steady her, he said, "Your wish is my command."

And it was.

# Epilogue

Andrew Cavanaugh's house was teeming with family members. All his family members. The former chief of police hadn't merely extended an invitation this time, as was his habit—he had *instructed* everyone to come, telling them to do whatever they had to in order to change their schedule and make themselves available for a family gathering.

When his oldest son had pressed him why it was so important to have everyone there, Andrew had said that he would understand when the time came.

"Anyone know what this is about?" Patrick Cavanaugh asked, scanning the faces of his cousins, or as many as he could see from his position in his uncle's expanded family room. There seemed to be family as far as the eye could see, spilling into the kitchen and parts beyond.

Callie, standing closest to her cousin, shook her head. "Not a clue."

Rayne moved closer to her oldest sister, not an easy feat these days given her condition. Rayne was carrying twins whom she referred to as miniature gypsies, given their continuous restless state.

"Maybe he's decided, since there're so many of us, that we're forming our own country and seceding from the union," she quipped. Rayne laced her fingers through her husband's as she added, "You never know with Dad."

Kansas looked at Ethan and briefly entertained the idea—knowing that the Cavanaugh patriarch celebrated each family occasion with a party—that this might be because she and Ethan were engaged. So far, it was a secret. Or was it?

"You didn't tell him, did you?" she whispered to Ethan.

Ethan shook his head, but the same thought had crossed his mind, as well. If not for the way the "invitation" had been worded, he wouldn't have ruled out the possibility.

"From what I hear," he whispered back, "there's never a need to tell the man anything. He always just seems to know things."

They heard Brian laugh and realized that the chief of detectives had somehow gotten directly behind them. "Despite the rumors, my older brother's not a psychic," Brian told them, highly amused.

This was the first opportunity Kansas had had to see the man since Bonner's capture. In all the ensuing action, she hadn't had a chance to tell him how grateful she was that he had come to her aid. Rescuing obviously ran in the family, she mused.

Turning around to face Brian, Kansas said, "I really want to thank you, Chief, for putting in a good word for me with the Crime Scene Investigation Unit."

"All I was doing was rubber-stamping a very good idea," he told her, brushing off her thanks.

Brian had been instrumental in bringing up her name to the head of the unit. He'd done it to save her the discomfort of going back to the firehouse and trying to work with people who regarded her with hostility because she'd turned in one of their own.

Seeing her smile of relief was payment enough for him. "Thank *you* for agreeing to join the CSI unit. They're damn lucky to have you," he told her with feeling. "Hopefully, you'll decide to stay with the department after Captain Lawrence comes to his senses and asks you to reconsider your resignation."

Kansas shook her head. She sincerely doubted that Captain Lawrence would ever want her back. He all but came out and said so, commenting that he felt she would be "happier someplace else." And he was right. She felt she'd finally found a home. In more ways than one.

"You have nothing to worry about there." Things had gotten very uncomfortable for her within the firehouse after Bonner was caught and arraigned. Everyone agreed that Bonner should be held accountable for what he'd done, but the bad taste the whole case had generated wasn't going to go away anytime soon. And it was primarily focused on her.

Transferring to another fire station wouldn't help. Her "reputation" would only follow her. She would always be the outsider, the investigator who turned on her own. She'd had no choice but to resign. The moment she had, like an answer to a prayer, Brian Cavanaugh had come to her with an offer from the Crime Scene Investigation unit. The division welcomed her with open arms.

"Good. I know I speak for all the divisions when I say that we look forward to working with you on a regular basis."

About to add something further, Brian fell silent as he saw his older brother walk into the center of the room. He, along with Lila and Rose, were the only other people who knew what was going on—if he didn't count the eight people waiting to walk into the room.

This, Brian thought, was going to knock everyone's proverbial socks off.

"Everybody, if I could have your attention," Andrew requested, raising his deep baritone voice so that he could be heard above the din of other conversations. Silence swiftly ensued as all eyes turned toward him.

"What's with the melodrama, Dad?" Rayne, his youngest and a card-carrying rebel until very recently, wanted to know, putting the question to him that was on everyone else's mind.

"No melodrama," Andrew assured her. "I just wanted all of you to hear this at the same time so I wouldn't wind up having to repeat myself several dozen times. And so no one could complain that they were the last to know." He was looking directly at Rayne as he said it.

If she was going to say anything else, it would have to wait. Because Ethan scooped her into his arms and kissed her. And he intended to go on kissing her for a very long time to come.

\* \* \* \* \*

*Don't miss the next romance by* USA TODAY
*bestselling author Marie Ferrarella,*
*THE SHERIFF'S CHRISTMAS SURPRISE,*
*available November 2010*
*from Harlequin American Romance.*

# COMING NEXT MONTH

## Available September 28, 2010

**#1627 COVERT CHRISTMAS**
*Open Season* by Marilyn Pappano
*Second-Chance Sheriff* by Linda Conrad
*Saving Christmas* by Loreth Anne White

**#1628 DR. COLTON'S HIGH-STAKES FIANCÉE**
*The Coltons of Montana*
**Cindy Dees**

**#1629 PROFILE FOR SEDUCTION**
*The Cordasic Legacy*
**Karen Whiddon**

**#1630 THE BRIDE'S BODYGUARD**
*The Bancroft Brides*
**Beth Cornelison**

ROMANTIC SUSPENSE

# REQUEST YOUR
# FREE BOOKS!

## 2 FREE NOVELS
## PLUS
## 2 FREE GIFTS!

**ROMANTIC**

*S U S P E N S E*

*Sparked by Danger, Fueled by Passion.*

---

**YES!** Please send me 2 FREE Silhouette® Romantic Suspense novels and my 2 FREE gifts (gifts are worth about $10). After receiving them, if I don't wish to receive any more books, I can return the shipping statement marked "cancel." If I don't cancel, I will receive 4 brand-new novels every month and be billed just $4.24 per book in the U.S. or $4.99 per book in Canada. That's a saving of 15% off the cover price! It's quite a bargain! Shipping and handling is just 50¢ per book.* I understand that accepting the 2 free books and gifts places me under no obligation to buy anything. I can always return a shipment and cancel at any time. Even if I never buy another book from Silhouette, the two free books and gifts are mine to keep forever.

240/340 SDN E5Q4

| | |
|---|---|
| Name | |
| | (PLEASE PRINT) |

| | |
|---|---|
| Address | Apt. # |

| | | |
|---|---|---|
| City | State/Prov. | Zip/Postal Code |

Signature (if under 18, a parent or guardian must sign)

### Mail to the **Silhouette Reader Service:**
### **IN U.S.A.:** P.O. Box 1867, Buffalo, NY 14240-1867
### **IN CANADA:** P.O. Box 609, Fort Erie, Ontario L2A 5X3

Not valid for current subscribers to Silhouette Romantic Suspense books.

### **Want to try two free books from another line?**
### **Call 1-800-873-8635 or visit www.morefreebooks.com.**

* Terms and prices subject to change without notice. Prices do not include applicable taxes. N.Y. residents add applicable sales tax. Canadian residents will be charged applicable provincial taxes and GST. Offer not valid in Quebec. This offer is limited to one order per household. All orders subject to approval. Credit or debit balances in a customer's account(s) may be offset by any other outstanding balance owed by or to the customer. Please allow 4 to 6 weeks for delivery. Offer available while quantities last.

---

**Your Privacy:** Silhouette is committed to protecting your privacy. Our Privacy Policy is available online at www.eHarlequin.com or upon request from the Reader Service. From time to time we make our lists of customers available to reputable third parties who may have a product or service of interest to you. If you would prefer we not share your name and address, please check here. ☐

**Help us get it right**—We strive for accurate, respectful and relevant communications. To clarify or modify your communication preferences, visit us at www.ReaderService.com/consumerschoice.

SRS10R

*See below for a sneak peek at
our inspirational line, Love Inspired®.
Introducing HIS HOLIDAY BRIDE
by bestselling author Jillian Hart*

Autumn Granger gave her horse rein to slide toward the town's new sheriff.

"Hey, there." The man in a brand-new Stetson, black T-shirt, jeans and riding boots held up a hand in greeting. He stepped away from his four-wheel drive with "Sheriff" in black on the doors and waded through the grasses. "I'm new around here."

"I'm Autumn Granger."

"Nice to meet you, Miss Granger. I'm Ford Sherman, from Chicago." He knuckled back his hat, revealing the most handsome face she'd ever seen. Big blue eyes contrasted with his sun-tanned complexion.

"I'm guessing you haven't seen much open land. Out here, you've got to keep an eye on cows or they're going to tear your vehicle apart."

"What?" He whipped around. Sure enough, mammoth black-and-white creatures had started to gnaw on his four-wheel drive. They clustered like a mob, mouths and tongues and teeth bent on destruction. One cow tried to pry the wiper off the windshield, another chewed on the side mirror. Several leaned through the open window, licking the seats.

"Move along, little dogie." He didn't know the first thing about cattle.

The entire herd swiveled their heads to study him curiously. Not a single hoof shifted. The animals soon returned to chewing, licking, digging through his possessions.

Autumn laughed, a warm and wonderful sound. "Thanks,

I needed that." She then pulled a bag from behind her saddle and waved it at the cows. "Look what I have, guys. Cookies."

Cows swung in her direction, and dozens of liquid brown eyes brightened with cookie hopes. As she circled the car, the cattle bounded after her. The earth shook with the force of their powerful hooves.

"Next time, you're on your own, city boy." She tipped her hat. The cowgirl stayed on his mind, the sweetest thing he had ever seen.

*Will Ford be able to stick it out in the country
to find out more about Autumn?
Find out in HIS HOLIDAY BRIDE
by bestselling author Jillian Hart,
available in October 2010
only from Love Inspired®.*